A Thousand Cranes for India

THE INDIA LIST

A Thousand Cranes for India

RECLAIMING PLURALITY AMID HATRED

EDITED BY
PALLAVI AIYAR

LONDON NEW YORK CALCUTTA

Seagull Books, 2020

Texts © Individual contributors
This compilation © Seagull Books

ISBN 978 0 8574 2 744 1

British Library Cataloguing-in-Publication Data
A catalogue record for this book is available from the British Library

Typeset and designed by Sunandini Banerjee, Seagull Books, Calcutta, India
Printed and bound by Hyam Enterprises, Calcutta, India

For Bhaia
who's always fought the good fight

.

in folding paper
there are mountains and valleys . . .
cranes flying home

Kawaguchi Hitoshi

*I, who have the amphibious duality of nature in me, whose food is in the
West and breathe air in the East, do not find a place where I can build my
nest. I suppose I shall have to be a migratory bird and cross and recross
the sea, owning two nests, one on each shore.*

Rabindranath Tagore

CONTENTS

A Thousand Cranes for India

PALLAVI AIYAR

I was on a family holiday in Hiroshima when I read, on my phone, about Asifa Bano. The eight-year-old's kidnapping, protracted confinement in a temple, gangrape and murder was an item in the news digest that popped up in my email inbox every morning.

It's a benumbed world. I was accustomed to digesting news of rapes along with breakfast toast; to imbibing images of death with my ginger and brown-sugar-sweetened coffee. But this time my body revolted. I'm not sure why. There were always so many atrocities in competition. If I could not be equally outraged by every brutality—and we seemed to have such a wellspring of these—was it fair to be outraged by any one?

I was Indian. Every breath could, would I permit it to, give me cause for anger, pause for the searing injustices of the quotidian. I could be vexed that while my maid's alcoholic husband beat her at night, my greatest problem was choosing which Netflix series to watch. I could take umbrage at the fact that a few hundred metres down from where my children rehearsed for their piano recital, there were babies sitting over open gutters, flies in their eyes and little but air in their bloated bellies. I might be incensed that a Muslim colleague couldn't find anyone willing to rent him an apartment, or that despite my 'liberal' ways I had no Dalit friends. In

India, there was injustice in simply being alive, but to be alive to injustice was to be unable to live.

And yet, on the day that I read about how Asifa Bano was sedated, violated, bludgeoned and choked, my usual reaction to events like this—horror comfortingly underlain by an awareness of its own ephemerality—was supplanted by a dense weight that I feared would never lift. I was winded, emptied of words, stripped of succour.

Asifa had sparkling eyes. She had ponytails and an impish smile. On the day she was taken, she'd been out grazing her family's horses in a meadow. She was wearing a purple dress. A man had beckoned her into a forest, and because she was a child, and children tend to trust and obey adults, she followed him. She was then force-fed drugs, dragged to a nearby temple and locked in. Over the next several days, she was raped again and again by multiple men, including the temple priest and a number of police officers.[1] She was starved, beaten and eventually strangled.

If only this were the end. But when it came to Asifa the debasement was infinite. When the police arrested the accused, protests broke out in *defence* of the alleged rapists. Groups of lawyers and politicians tried to prevent the police from entering the court to file charges.

---

1 On 10 June 2019, a special court convicted three of the eight charge-sheeted men to life imprisonment: Sanji Ram, the temple priest, Parvesh Kumar, a friend of the priests' nephew and Deepak Khajuria, a police officer. Three other police officers were sentenced to five years' imprisonment for destroying evidence. Sanji Ram's son was acquitted, given 'the benefit of the doubt'. At the time of publishing, the trial of the eighth accused, a nephew of Sanji Ram, is pending as the process of determining whether he is a juvenile continues.

As it turned out, Asifa's rape and murder had not even primarily been about her. Her brutalization was incidental, a diverting means to an end. It was but a salvo in the attempt to terrorize the community she belonged to, a nomadic group of Muslim shepherds called Bakarwals, out of the area, so that it could remain pristinely Hindu. It was an evil concatenation of every ugliness: misogyny, religious bigotry, majoritarianism. It had happened in a temple. There were people who had celebrated it. It felt like a declaration of war, on the powerless, on India, on me. How was I to respond?

All morning, I didn't speak of what I had learnt. I held it close to me, like a dirty secret in which I was complicit. It was not my hands that had choked the life out of the girl, nor my body that had penetrated her's so violently as to rip her uterus. And yet it had happened on my watch, in my country. I was alive; she was not.

That morning, with my husband and boys—ages six and nine—I visited the sprawling Peace Park memorial to the victims of the August 1945 nuclear bombing, the fulcrum of Hiroshima's tourist itinerary. It was intended as a quick stop before departing for the more salubrious Torii gate-framed beauty of Miyajima Island. Truth be told, wallowing in memories of maimed atomic bomb victims was not high on my planned agenda.

Most estimates put the number of those who'd been killed instantaneously by the bombing at between 60,000 and 80,000. The heat generated was so intense that some people had simply vanished in the explosion. Tens of thousands more died of the long-term effects of radiation and the final death toll is currently calculated at between 120,000 and 140,000.

As we walked through and around the space, its hall of remembrance, bridges, ponds, cenotaph and gardens aflame with spring flowers, the statistics felt hollow. I was unable to shake off the feeling of Asifa Bano walking next to me. Her eyes were without accusation, only wide with curiosity, as she took in the artefacts on display.

At the memorial museum we looked at 'School Trousers', a wretchedly tattered pair that belonged to Naoki Mikami, a young boy attending morning assembly in his schoolyard at the moment of the explosion. He died four hours after managing to stagger back home. Later we stood silently in front of a piece of 'White Wall Stained by the Black Rain'. The 'black rain' was the radioactive dust and soot mixed with water vapour that fell on Hiroshima soon after the bomb was detonated. The heaviness I had felt since the morning was fed and fattened by the black-and-white portraits of the survivors and their testimonies.

But then we came upon two unadorned paper cranes, gentle and defiant. They seemed to acknowledge the horror but refuse the ugliness. These were not the first origami cranes I had seen in Hiroshima. The city was festooned in skeins of them. They hung in front of okonomiyaki pancake restaurants and sat in gift-shop windows. From schoolchildren to world leaders, people from around the world folded and sent in millions of these birds to the city every year.

The reason for this global flight of paper cranes originated in a tragedy where the victim, like Asifa, was a little girl. Sadako Sasaki was two years old when she stared uncomprehendingly at the giant mushroom cloud slowly blotting out the sky. She survived, but would not live long; she died a decade on, in great pain, of radiation-related leukaemia. Lying sick in the hospital, Sadoko had desperately folded origami cranes in hopes of a reprieve, for according to a Japanese legend, those who fold a thousand paper cranes will have their prayers answered. The young girl folded and shaped her birds, but her strength gave out and she died. Yet, her cranes took wing.

They have since emerged as a symbol of apology, healing and resistance. Of renewal in the face of devastation, atonement for the horrors inflicted by our own, and of warning that we must remember, so as not to repeat. They may have emerged out of Japan's particular mythology and history, but they belong to no one nation. The crane is a migratory bird; it crosses borders and makes its home with scant regard to the blood-soaked lines that humans have drawn on maps.

Later that day I tried my hand at folding a paper crane for the first time. Asifa was still by my side, but the meditative, solemn care needed to make and unmake the creases eased something in me. It was as if I were folding in the depravities of the world and transforming them into a weightless being of beauty. I released my crane down a chute from the twelfth floor of the Orizu Tower, a building adjacent to the Peace Museum. It swirled down: light as a wish, strong as a pledge. And I was determined in that moment not to lose the war begat by Asifa's murderers and others like them who killed and raped in the name of piety or purity. I would fight for my India using the only weapons I had: words and cranes.

Back in Tokyo, I began to post pictures of paper cranes on social media. I made a video asking people to fold cranes as a gesture of defiance, an act of reclamation.

My India was a country held together not by geography, language or ethnicity but by an idea: an idea that asserted, even celebrated, multiplicity.

I was a mongrel: a Delhiite, an English speaker; half a Tamilian, half a UP-wali; culturally a Hindu; by choice an atheist; by heritage a Muslim. But the identity that threaded these multiplicities together was at once the most powerful and most amorphous: I was an Indian.

This India, my India, was besieged, still it lived. People responded to the appeal and sent me pictures of their cranes. I received images of mangled birds and perfectly articulated ones; cranes placed on top of kitchen counters and car dashboards. They flew into my inbox from Jakarta, Beijing, Tokyo, California, Mumbai, Bangalore, Pune, Hong Kong, Chennai, Delhi.

I began to brainstorm with my friend, literary agent and crane-folder, Jayapriya Vasudevan. These conversations birthed the idea for this book, for using the paper crane as a motif of connection and beauty in an otherwise degraded milieu, for enabling those of us who fought with words to reach out to each other and become the best army we could be. We could not bring Asifa back, but the collective beating of the wings of our cranes would be a gauntlet to those who would bludgeon our capacious civilization into the confines of their grotesquely narrow notion of India.

The twenty-three pieces in this book encompass reportage, stories, poems, memoir and polemic: the kind of complex and enriching diversity that India demands and deserves. In some of them, the cranes are like Easter eggs, almost hidden from sight, their meaning in need of excavation. In Prajwal Parajuly's essay, 'The Tenant', the fault lines of class and region are unpacked through the dynamic between Parajuly's Sikkim-based parents and their Rajasthani migrant tenant, Deepak. A mobile of paper cranes dangles from the balcony ceiling of Deepak's rented apartment, an attempt, futile and hopeful, to assert his ownership over the space.

In Anjum Hasan's meditation on the possibilities and contradictions of womanhood, 'Love on the Delhi Metro', an unnamed narrator riding in the ladies' compartment of the Indian capital's metro muses about her determination to refuse the categories imposed by gender, only to be confounded by the sight of a child playing with a paper crane.

Veena Venugopal's story, 'The Maid', skewers the hypocrisies and inequalities of the servant–mistress relationship with a social-media twist: 'My son learnt to make origami cranes in school. Look at all our attempts. Of course, the best cranes are my maid Mili's.'

Cranes take centre stage in essays written by both Salil Tripathi and Swaminathan Aiyar, but not the origami varieties; in 'The Siberian Crane Doesn't Live Here Any More', and 'Requiem for the Siberian Crane', the veteran journalists use the early twenty-first century disappearance of the migratory Siberian crane from north India's plain's as a metaphor for the increasing hostility of the Indian landscape to 'outsiders'. Tripathi's essay ends with a vision of hope: 'Look at the sky; drops of water are making our faces wet. Rain is falling. Cranes are flying.'

Aiyar's conclusion is more sombre. Subverting Rabindranath Tagore, he writes of today's India: 'It is a place where the mind is full of fear and the head is held discreetly low; where knowledge is too dangerous to be shared freely; where the country has deliberately been broken into fragments by narrow domestic walls of religion; where words come out of the depths of opportunism; where tireless striving stretches its arms towards communalism; where the clear stream of reason has been told to go take a "sickular" hike; into that cesspit of unfreedom, my father, has my country fallen.'

In Jonathan Gil Harris' memoir, '(Un)Folding Secrets: The Contents of My Mother's Chinese Chest', folding becomes a powerful metaphor. 'I too am folding here: folding, if not a crane, then a story out of bits of stray paper from the Chinese chest [...] in the hope of connecting with a larger family I never knew, and in the hope of reconstituting something of what was shattered by the war.'

Harris' essay shifts across time and geography from New Zealand to Warsaw, Central Asia and Delhi, arguing that the act of unfolding the pain and secrets we fold away in our lifetimes is necessary to confront the venom of hatred.

Several of the other contributors range globally as well, even as they take India as their starting or end points. In 'The Silence of the Crane', Radhika Jha talks about the dangers of silence, referencing incidents both historical and personal, from the Armenian genocide in the Ottoman Empire to her own experiences in modern-day Goa.

Ranjit Hoskote's 'Travelling in the Zone' is a contemplation of photojournalists 'reaping the wages of destruction and the arrears of hope' across the world and through the decades. He concludes: 'I picture many hands tearing these images of anguish from magazines and newspapers, and folding them into paper cranes. I picture a flight of paper cranes, thousands of them, gliding across lines of control and no-fly zones.'

Samrat Chowdhury's piece, 'Aziz from Pakistan', returns this book to Hiroshima, a city he travels to with a Pakistani acquaintance who is wrought into a friend by the shared experiences and conversations of the journey. 'Compassion and kindness are inherently human traits. The children from around the world who send a steady stream of origami cranes, millions of them, with their wishes of peace year after year, are just ordinary kids being kids,' says Samrat. But what exactly does 'peace' mean? Is it just the absence of war? Samrat disagrees.

Shovon Chowdhury's story, 'The Magic Pants', brings to this anthology a dose of comic wryness. In it a dour, frustrated group of right-wing RSS functionaries glimpse happiness by improving their dress sense and learning to flirt with women by teaching them how to fold paper cranes.

Conversely, Sudeep Chakravarti's 'Art of War' is a sharp counterpoint in tone. He describes the clinical barbarity displayed by the State as it attempts to force those who disagree with it back to the so-called 'democratic fold'. 'The Inuit have several descriptions for snow, I have a few for razor wire,' Chakravarti says. The concentric circles of wire surrounding the base of the anti-Maoist operation in western Bengal that he reports from are like an installation, 'you could easily place a string of white origami cranes on to juxtapose the reality of violence to a quixotic yearning for peace.

Writer and filmmaker Natasha Badhwar's essay knits together the personal with the political as she chronicles her travels with Karwan e Mohabbat, a civil-society initiative that involves visiting and listening to the families of victims of hate crimes. Badhwar's first-born daughter accompanies her on many of these journeys, watching silently. At home, her middle daughter is left to deal with her anxieties about the world, while her youngest child folds tiny paper cranes with which to welcome the birth of a cousin. The baby is transformative, bringing with it the one commodity that has been in short supply: hope. Badhwar writes: 'Acting as if we have hope gives us hope and eventually averts our own surrender to despair.'

Cranes weave in and out of every piece in this collection. But I will end this introduction by leaving the last words to some of our poets, as should be the case, always:

We know, don't we, that a forest is being
truncheoned as we speak? That a girl in that forest
is being truncheoned too. A girl, or a hundred.

—Tishani Doshi, 'Why the Brazilian Butt Lift Won't Save Us'

Only the smallest gesture and the gentlest act
Redeem our lives against the falling of the sand.

—Tabish Khair, 'Folded Paper: A Ghazal'

Why the Brazilian Butt Lift Won't Save Us

TISHANI DOSHI

The body refuses happiness.
That was *once upon a time*,
that was long ago when you could run naked
through a field without consternation.
You and your perfectly sized baby parts.

The body grows dissatisfied
once it starts towering over dogs
and staring into the hearts of kitchen counters.

Pretty soon your alter-body
is calling from a downtown phone booth
saying, Listen, baby, you need to step up the retinoids.

We know, don't we, that a forest is being
truncheoned as we speak? That a girl in that forest
is being truncheoned too. A girl, or a hundred.
That all the words we have for *my heart can't take
it any more* won't be able to describe
what happens to the body at the end of that.

Still, the body wants to be glorious while it can.

It sees lips burgeoning like a Hokusai wave,
and thinks, I'll have some of that. It sees bones Caravaggio
might have dreamed of and micro-bladed eyebrows
and neat marble apples the size of a generously cupped hand,
and says, yes, yes, yes. But mostly, it sees
Kim Kardashian's ass rising like a mountain
out of the Atlantic, and thinks, I, too,
want to oversee a metropolis.

And why shouldn't it?

Aren't we all trying to get back to a time
before the blemishes? When the body was
a carefree skeleton with no stretch marks
and pristine platelet-rich hair—
an origami crane built to withstand
the damaging effects of light,
gusting on thermals to fly
against any mushroom cloud.

So what's a few small wounds to the forehead?
What's a needle the size of your life?

The Siberian Crane
Doesn't Live Here Any More

SALIL TRIPATHI

The last Siberian cranes came to Keoladeo National Park (as the Bharatpur Bird Sanctuary is now known) in the winter of 2001, or perhaps 2002. Nobody is quite sure. But at some point, as the soft, pale light struggled to cut through the thick smog enveloping the skies over northern India, the birds stopped visiting India.

Scientists have suggested reasons, including the possibility that the Siberian crane might now be extinct. I am not a scientist, and I remain struck by the timing when the cranes stopped flying to India. For 2002 was the year of a carnage in Gujarat that lasted months. First a train was set on fire in Godhra on 28 February 2002, in which 58 people perished. Many of the passengers on the train were karsevaks, determined to erect a temple to replace a mosque, which had already been destroyed in the distant town of Ayodhya in 1992. Word spread quickly that such a vile deed—the burning of the train in Godhra, not the destruction of the mosque ten years earlier—could only have been done by *those* people. And the chief minister of the state at that time, who had been in power for a few months, did not immediately ask the army to patrol the streets; instead he allowed the dead bodies to be brought to one of Gujarat's main cities, Ahmedabad, its journey planting seeds of hatred that erupted promptly and inevitably, and in the days that followed, *these* people took revenge on *those* people, and officially nearly 900 people died—but unofficially, who knows?

Instead of the white cranes with their black feathers, the skies over Gujarat's cities were filled with vultures.

Cranes fly in a formation like an arrow; only ballerinas can hope to imitate their graceful movements. The vultures, black and dark, are different. They come to feast. They wait near a starving child, too weak to flee, till the child collapses. (Kevin Carter, who took a haunting photograph of such a scene and won the Pulitzer Prize for it in 1993, took his own life within a year.) The vultures looked like military jets hovering over a city that was to be bombed. But bombs from the sky weren't necessary—the people were doing the killings themselves. Ehsan Jafri, a trade unionist and politician slain during that massacre, wrote this poem, which I first heard in Sheena Sumaria's film about the massacres, *Even the Crows*:

> Neither the leaders nor the protectors came to rescue him
> He was chased down the street, daggers in their hands
> When he knocked on the kind people's doors
> He found his slayers.
> We worshipped the sun and moon at home
> Worthless rocks they turned out to be
> His corpse lay rotting on the streets
> Even the crows turned out to be better than humans.

The crows stayed away; the vultures remained; the cranes never returned.

*

I knew another kind of crane when I lived in Singapore. These cranes were tall, like the giraffe, and made of metal. They were shiny—usually yellow, sometimes red, often green or blue. They lifted materials and built cities across Asia. The joke in Singapore then was: 'What is the national bird of Singapore?' 'The crane.'

These cranes were ungainly. They attempted to simulate the movements of elbows and other body parts, but they had to struggle hard to recreate the grace of the human form. They were clunky and noisy. They could not operate on some surfaces—bulldozers often had to precede them to level the ground. The people who worked the cranes had to wear masks to keep out the dust, put on glasses to protect their eyes and don helmets to guard their heads. These men, and they were usually men, built highways in Singapore, condominiums in Jakarta and the world's tallest office towers in Kuala Lumpur. They had come from elsewhere—like those migratory birds. Cities in Asia suffered from an edifice complex; becoming taller and reaching higher meant becoming stronger in those days. It was an Asian disease—as if the only values Asians understood were property values.

I didn't see many birds then. In Singapore, the government had a group of armed men who shot down crows. Their constant caw-cawing were assumed by the authorities to annoy foreign investors and tourists. To see birds you had to go to a bird park. To listen to them sing you went to Chinatown, where old men taught birds in cages how to sing. This was the island of contrived entertainment.

I did see many aeroplanes though. The Singapore Air Force's jets streamed across the sky, leaving behind magnificent trails, in an attempt to imitate the formation of cranes, but never quite succeeding. For the cranes flew, leaving an impression in the mind's eye; the trails of the jets' fumes dissipated, disappearing into the blue sky. More jets crowded the airspace, looking like giant prehistoric birds, before they too were no longer visible. My sons, who were young then, would often be joined by their friends in a little game. The boys would stare at the planes and play a game of 'guess the airline' by spotting the logos on their tails.

It was bird-watching for the modern era.

This was the future that India wanted—to become a busy country where planes take off and land all the time, where children would learn the planes by their tails, and not the birds by their sounds. This was the Asia that was leaving India behind; an Asia that had already discovered the magic of the market and was headed in the direction that India was so keen to follow.

To get there, India would need bulldozers—and cranes, though not the kind that had considered India their home, but the kind that would make India into something it hadn't been.

*

I had seen the Siberian crane once, in the mid-1990s. I was on vacation in India with my family in Bharatpur. Our guide was an old man who took us around on a cycle rickshaw, pedalling slowly, showing us egrets, teals, storks, spoonbills and hornbills, until we reached an open space with a large pond of water in the far distance. A bunch of eager men and women stood along the path, training their binoculars to explore the surface of the pond, shushing us into silence. We got off the vehicle to try and see what they were looking at.

The forest was silent. A mild breeze caressed us. We kept looking, still not sure what we were waiting for. I asked a woman in a white panama hat standing next to us. 'Shhh,' she began, then noticing my sons, who were eight and five at that time, she said, 'Siberian crane. There are a few somewhere near, and they should be here any time soon. Be quiet.'

I looked around—the group of bird-watchers was a microcosm of India—Parsis and Sikhs I could identify easily, but the others didn't wear their identities on their dress or sleeves. We weren't there to learn about the distinction that class makes and caste perpetuates. At the end of the day we'd all go our separate ways, but at the moment we were part of this adventure, looking out for the Siberian crane.

'There it is,' a jovial man shouted, his finger raised to the east, and all the binoculars swung in that direction. Hurrahs rang out, and there was applause.

We had identified the birds that sought comfort in a warmer India. They had fled from the frigid Arctic north, looking for refuge. In those days India was open. It did not ask the birds if they ate this or that fish or insect, or if they were vegetarian, or whether they believed in one divine being or many. The answers did not need to be approved before the birds were allowed to enter Indian airspace. For India then was wide enough, large enough, open enough and broad-minded enough to let the birds fly in each winter and back home in spring.

Refugees had done that in India too—the ten million who came from East Pakistan in March 1971 had returned home within months of their country's liberation in December 1971, returning home as Bangladeshis. India had always kept its doors open for others fleeing persecution— Tibetans who couldn't return to Tibet; Tamils from Sri Lanka who faced massacres in their country; Afghans who had enough of their wars and felt unsafe in Pakistan; Burmese escaping from the generals, and later a small number of Rohingyas, who couldn't trust the civilians in charge in Myanmar either. Everyone got refuge in India, even Stalin's estranged daughter.

India was an aviary which had room for every bird, every nest; it had its own birds, and they mingled and flew together creating rich murmurations, and India took in more birds, keeping its windows and doors wide open, so that the breeze from everywhere could come in and continue to reinvigorate the land. It was a confident India, not suspicious, not feeling inferior. Rabindranath Tagore hated barriers and borders, which were artificial and created from above, dividing people, forcing them to require permits to cross frontiers. Mohandas Gandhi agreed with the poet, even though he wanted his feet to be planted firmly on Indian soil. That showed a difference of opinion, but it wasn't fundamental: neither wanted to close the windows and shut the doors, because their India was confident—it was a civilization, not merely a country; a subcontinent, not a mere nation; it was, as Jawaharlal Nehru knew, 'some ancient palimpsest on which layer upon layer of thought and reverie had been inscribed, and yet no succeeding layer had completely hidden or erased what had been written previously.'

Cranes were welcome; they didn't need passports.

But India began to change in 2002. And the cranes stopped coming.

*

Crane. C R A N E. C Rane. Rain. See Rain.

India is the land of heat and dust. But it is also the land where it rains. The rain is pleasant, the water not so cold; the temperature dips but not so low that you have to bring out sweaters, and it is possible to venture out in it armed with a sturdy umbrella. Think Raj Kapoor and Nargis, looking into each other's eyes in a black-and-white movie, walking under an umbrella on a wet evening. But rain can be tragic too—like the downpour that lured Durga, who discovered the joy of swaying in the water, getting wet, her hair swinging wildly, while her brother Apu watched her gay abandon unaware that the torrent would consume her.

The lush grass sways as the wind rushes through the field unannounced and invisible, the dark clouds resound with thunder a few moments after a streak of lightning has lit up the sky. The pied crested cuckoo, the *chaataka*, sings, the peacock dances, the rain comforts the parched ground. The undulating rhythm of wipers clearing car windscreens in Bombay. The smell by the seaside of roasted corn on the cob, sprinkled with salt, lime and chilli.

This land has stayed arid for long. The cranes have gone away. It hasn't rained. The temperature needs cooling.

*

Joseph Stalin died in 1953. In the political thaw that followed in what used to be the Soviet Union, films got made and novels got written where writers and filmmakers explored the boundaries that were being redrawn, to understand better what was now possible to say and what still remained off limits. In 1957, Mikhail Kalatozov made a film called *Letiat Zhuravli*

(*The Cranes Are Flying*), which would win the Palme d'Or at the Cannes Film Festival the following year. It was a moving love story with undertones that allegorically lifted the lid on emotions and ideas suppressed during the Stalin years.

Rather than follow the didactic social-realist style that had become the norm in the Soviet Union, Kalatozov allowed the visuals to do the talking—from the early spring in the footsteps of the young lovers, to the protagonist Veronica's determination to find out what happened to her lover Boris, who had enlisted for the war.

The film opened and closed with the image of cranes flying in formation. They flew in freedom and there were no limits in the sky. The lovers below too hopped around the city way past midnight, in a city without people, without traffic, without anyone—asserting their freedom—freedoms that Stalin had denied; freedoms that they believed could finally be regained.

The cranes flew free at the beginning of the film, but soon tanks started trundling along the streets. Veronica went on to experience the pains of a lifetime during the war—the loss of her lover, a return home to find her apartment complex razed, with no signs of her parents, a betrayal, and a rape. But finally, there was redemption. And cranes would fly once again.

Years later, Stalin's daughter would flee the clutches of the Soviet Union to seek freedom, and she would seek asylum. In India.

*

In Hiroshima, as if in an act of atonement, of penance, of meditation, you can make cranes from paper. Without a single cut, only by folding, small sheets of paper assume the shape of cranes, carrying hopes of a better world. Those cranes heal.

Other cranes aim to build, but they also raze—they seize land, they transform the landscape.

That din and dust scare the cranes that fly. They have stopped flying.

But the searing heat that has cracked the soil and dried the landscape, making it arid, will one day disappear. When the breeze blows again, as surely it will, the trees will shiver and flags will flutter and lights will shimmer, and the cranes, even those of paper, will begin to spread their wings and you might think the monsoon is close. And then a night of cold wind, banging windows, and swirling dust will bring the rain, and in the morning, all of a sudden, the land will turn greener.

There will be rain again, and the cranes will come. Gandhi said: 'When I despair, I remember that all through history the way of truth and love have always won. There have been tyrants and murderers, and for a time, they can seem invincible, but in the end, they always fall. Remember this—always.'

Look at the sky; drops of water are making our faces wet. Rain is falling. Cranes are flying.

Love on the Delhi Metro

ANJUM HASAN

I happen to glance down and notice that the big toe on her left foot is missing, a muted stump instead. *Darling, what have you done to yourself?* She has that colour in her cheeks that comes from a milk-fed prosperity, everlasting youth, self-absorbed happiness. The whole time that she stands there by the door and I stand there facing her, I am secretly cataloguing her beauty: the shimmer of her hair, the shine of her watch-strap, the gloss of her lips, the glow of her eyes, the opalescent earrings.

I love this about women—that left to themselves they become themselves and see nothing but themselves. Not just those who look into the flattering camera eye of their phones, not just those who study their reflections when the glass is darkened by the train's passage through tunnels, but all of them. All of us. Yet all of us have this too: the missing toe or some piece of our hearts that's mutilated, some prized and secret deformity or ghastly, visible scar. We are each straining towards something—a healing or a completion, a correction, a realignment.

The world is a difficult home for us; we build our half-secure rooms in it and fill them with all the comfort we can gather but it's not ever enough. There is always the voice calling from outside the window, the fist banging on the door. And then the train pulls into Model Town, Milkmaid gets off, a thickset man finds himself in this all-women compartment, looks mildly confused, is reminded of his gender, looks shocked, hurls himself out through the doors just as they are closing and stands there on the platform, forlorn. A wave of women has swarmed out, a wave of women swarm in, and a new perfume fills our locked female box, a new combination of skin and sweat, almost-empty lunch boxes and still-drying shampooed hair.

I share a seat with a woman who is typing on her phone. *Doc said there is no cure for morning sickness.* She looks tired, swollen, hungry. *So I just have to cope with it.* I can feel the warmth from her plump, bare arm seeping into my arm, her jean-clad thigh against my jean-clad thigh. Her swimming foetus and my empty womb. *She said to be patient. Time lagega.* Then she starts swiping through pictures of her husband and herself, impatient, lingering over none, seeking something that's not quite there, not in those pictures, not in the movement of this train which she doesn't seem to be going along with, nor in the faces of her co-travellers, at whom she never looks. She scowls at nothing, then shuts her eyes, and I feel as exhausted, I feel her exhaustion. I am weakened by my bleeding, dislike the shape of my knees, trying to love every new grey strand in my hair, troubled by the acutely mental pain in the small of my back, wish I could carry off rhinestone stilettos like the girl to my right or smilingly expose my navel like the tank-topped teenager standing before me. But at least I am not this— sick with motherhood. It would be like slipping into the narrative of a woman one likes, setting up home inside her, but then never being able to change one's mind and get the hell out of there. I've never liked my womanness enough to want to be saddled with it for life and what is this beside me—these swollen ankles, this creased forehead, this tenderness felt to breaking point—but an initiation into commitment for all eternity?

I read a story as a child about a woman who wakes up one morning and finds herself transformed into—no, not a bug, that was a man—but an ant. The world is henceforth to be ruled by ants and she is a queen ant, the slender body her lover cherished gone forever, bloated now to imperial proportions. She is going to spend all her time laying eggs while the other females scurry around feeding the larvae and defending the colony, and the males stand at attention, waiting to impregnate the queen and then die. What I remember best about that story is its wistfulness. The woman was glad to have this new life of female focus and yet missed the carefree indeterminacy of her previous one.

Time lagega. I congratulate myself on having got away even though I continue sitting right there, feeling gravid with Ms Gravid, sensing the weight of her expectancy on me as she dozes off, and then for some time even the announcements fade away and there is just all of us quiet together, knitting life by letting it make its bloodied way, stitch by stitch, through us, reading *The Secrets of Stenography* or *The Queen of Shadows*, thinking of dinner or mascara or, like the girl wearing an all-pink baseball cap with a panther embossed on it, not looking up from Candy Crush Saga for three-quarters of an hour.

Then Pink Panther sticks her phone—it has a translucent pink case with pink bunny ears—into the pocket of her pink drawstring trousers, and there is an image of a girl's face on her pink sling bag who opens and shuts her pink eyelashes every time Pink Panther moves. She is out at the university stop and a group of four students, all of them with cropped hair and dense lipstick, one of them in deliberately mismatched socks—stripes versus polka dots—and sandals that show them off, gets in discussing the laziness of one of their professors who dispensed with a big two-volume feminist classic in one PPT presentation. *One is not born, but rather becomes, woman.* They are sassy and outspoken, they are coming into their own, they grow up a little each afternoon on the train-ride home, but something about the newfound tenor of their voices makes all too obvious their worrying vulnerability. In that challenge to dowdy authority, that questioning of the canonized, that political vigilance, there is a beauty and a toughness, which though taken together is enormous, which though combined is revolutionary, may yet still not be enough. The tortuously slow and centuries-long progress through a man's world, driven at each stage by tireless petitioning, by vociferousness, by strident campaigns that demand a mile—equality, say—and get an inch—unisex yoga wear, say—leaving everyone hard-edged and flattened to the one-dimensionality of their principles. Given the length of this haul, I whisper to the girls who are reading the feminist classics, who are becoming women on the train-ride home, this is our only hope: that the beauty not just temper but transform the toughness. Plain, placard-waving indignation is utterly mediocre. If you can't say it in the highest prose, why say it? If you can't capture for the consciousness all the big bumps and hard knots of human ambivalence, why try? If you can't find the metaphor that elevates, why speak?

A woman dressed in turquoise and purple silk—she is voluptuous with colour—speaks. Or rather shouts. She is shouting at a man who stands between this segregated compartment and the next one, and he appears to have strayed a few feet too close to this women, shown some incommensurate interest. He could be an ordinary family man who happened to venture an innocent look, or he could be a rapist in his spare time, or he could be both. The angry woman—the turquoise is bruised now, the purple is livid—promises to have him beaten up, arrested, exposed, derided. *Maar maar ke . . . Tum jaise logon ko . . . Khabardar phir se . . . Sharam haya. . . .* She goes on for longer than seems necessary, much after the man has shrunk and melted back into the crowd, and then I realize she is not addressing only him but all men. *Arrogant bastards.* That's what she's saying. Superior and sneering or leering and leching or meddling and mansplaining. All women allow themselves, now and then, a great stab of clarifying hatred for men.

Hate on the Delhi Metro. Consider the brute facts: oceans of women brutalized every minute, forests of little girls trafficked every day, mountain-high spikes in crimes against the second sex, sky-filling cries of female pain from every corner of the land. Try living with that. And so I admire the crystal shattering ring of the Peacock's anger, her righteous rage. I see that she will only be heard if she raises her voice and that she will only be noticed in turquoise and purple, and that to reach a certain age is to reach the point of no return. She is the sort of woman who has long killed all the angels in the house, long perfected brusqueness with her husband and forthrightness with her sons, a woman who may be done with seeking sweet delight but at least is no longer subject to endless night.

An old woman gets in at Civil Lines and I surrender my seat. Her eyes are like two shiny coins rescued from the grey rubble of a lifetime of house-work. The world tilts back on its imperfect axis, all the lit flares die out and are replaced by the tempered warmth of dozing hearths, all the colour relaxes into pastel, all texture becomes cottony from which protrude comfortable folds of maternal fat, and I recall the lines of the poem: *I like old women / ugly women / mean women / they are the salt of the earth / they are not disgusted by / human waste . . . dictators clown around / come and go / hands stained with human blood / old women / get up at dawn / buy meat fruit bread / clean cook / stand on the street / arms folded silent . . . Hamlet flails in a snare / Faust plays a base and comic role / Raskolnikov strikes with an axe / old women are indestructible / they smile knowingly . . . cowardice and bravery / greatness and smallness / they see in their proper proportions / commensurate with the demands / of everyday life.*

That's you, old woman. She actually smiles back at me as if she were fully tuned into this: the language of the heart. I had once wanted to write a compendium of women's sadness. It would chronicle every disappointed ambition, every snuffed hope, every misplaced dream, every act of cunning and subterfuge, every speck of spit taken in the face, every female wile, every female compromise, all the petty struggles and estranging jealousies, all the bitching and snarling, all the cattiness and fishiness, each dewdrop and teardrop, everything. I would find a way to compress this history of grief into the empty doorway and the maple leaf. I didn't find a way and here I am now, considering the ironic smile of an old woman and knowing I could never do it justice. I just don't know what it's like. I don't mean the shrinking of the spirit, the slumping of the shoulders, the clenching of the vagina, the working of fingers to the bone, no, not all of that, which can be easily imagined even if never emulated. What I can't hope to capture is how one lives with and yet is not martyred by this: still waking up every dawn to buy meat-bread-fruit, going out to teach-nurse-clean-counsel-serve, still able to slow down, joke, sing, recount stories, run fingertips slowly across the faces of the half-deserving. Who knows where that comes from—that unsurpassable dignity, that quiet stoicism, that hard-won ordinariness. It will be outdated soon, a vestige of the manmade society we are trying to dismantle, and with it you'll be gone, old woman, and that light in your eyes that comes from seeing greatness and smallness in their proper proportions.

Old woman's gone already at Kashmiri Gate, and I'm watching a family of five, something about the tint of their cheeks and the crispness of their accents suggesting apples, valleys and chinar trees, boots, barbed wire and guns. A mother with a baby asleep in her arms, her other girl of about seven, an older woman who talks in a commanding tone, and between them a restless adolescent, the older woman's daughter. The smaller girl is dreaming and sometimes breaks out of her smiling reverie to try and draw her mother's attention to herself, but her mother, busy with talk and busy with baby, answers only in snatches this little girl's minor queries about the world. The adolescent is already almost a woman, already halfway into the conversation between her mother and aunt. She interjects, complains, disagrees. Her mother pauses, her eyes narrow and harden, and she snaps warningly at her daughter, trying to hem in this child-woman. She can see something there she doesn't like at all—a dangerous hunger for liberty in a world full of checkposts, curfew hours, battle lines. The girl responds by poking her elbows into her mother's ribs, stamping her foot, not giving in.

Another mother and daughter pair are arguing drolly. Mother says daughter is not to keep her eggs in the fridge; no, she can't keep them on the top shelf because that is too near the leftover dal; no, she can't keep them in the salad tray because that is too near the ginger; no, she can't keep them in the door because that is too near the milk cartons. She just does not want eggs in her fridge, they disgust her and interfere with her spotless vegetarianism. They laugh so much over their quarrel, it does not seem like one at all, just a way to reinforce how much they have in common rather than how little. Then they start talking about shopping. The English word 'shopping' makes the Hindi of their conversation modern and light-hearted, that and all the other innocuous nouns—*birthday*, *gift*, *Uber*, *husband*, *credit card*, *flight*, *US*, *India*. A woman in a flimsy red sari with its frilly end drawn over her head, dragging along two tousled toddlers, gets in at Chawri Bazaar, a beautiful young frightened face innocent of make-up, and I think: this one won't parry with her children over eggs and meat, this one won't be able to live with the aid of a handful of English nouns. But she is out of the house all the same, she is on the Delhi Metro, autonomous for the length of a few stops, on her own for a while, on her way. This train is a thing that moves and so, though closet-shaped, it is better than the other closets in which women are routinely cloistered. *They shut me up in Prose— / As when a little Girl / They put me in the Closet— / Because they liked me 'still'—*

I want to study this creature at length, make conjectures about the exact source of her courage, identify the reason for her hunted expression, but when I look for her again she has been replaced by a pair of tiny girls, their hair tightly drawn back into topknots which sharpen the already fragile outlines of their faces, who are on their day off—from being nannies to monstrously demanding infants, or cleaners of sulphurous restaurant loos, or unsentimental retailers of hurried sex in dirty-walled brothels, or proles wedged forever between the shelves of a neighbourhood supermarket. They have dressed up in their new palazzo pants, their tightest shirts, and they take up between them only as much space as a single, not necessarily bigger, but more well-to-do woman would occupy, as if space were a commodity they did not feel they had a claim on, an extravagance they cannot entirely afford, a luxury not guaranteed with the price they paid for their tickets.

They are, mouths parted, eyes wide, nailed with awe to their shared seat, watching a girl across the aisle with an overstuffed handbag from which she draws out the magical appurtenances of her tribe and deftly does up her face—eyelids, lips, cheeks, hair. For ten full minutes this tableau—two poor girls watching one rich girl watching herself make herself pretty. All I can think of saying to them if I could say something to them is—look at yourselves instead, give credit to who you are—but that would be a laughable lie for they know what's on top, what calls the shots, what sets the terms. I could snatch *The Art of Japanese Management* from the earnest, bespectacled girl who is reading the chapter titled 'Shoguns and Merchants' and give it to them, but they'd say they don't want my charity—they just want to become me. I could tell them they are tougher, clearer, wiser, sweeter and they would just look me up and down and say: *How much did you pay for that bracelet?*

At Rajiv Chowk they are swallowed by the city that created them and I am pressed up by the growing crush against three girls who are debating whether the recent Supreme Court repeal of the law that makes infidelity a crime is a good thing or bad. One says: *Women will get a free hand now. They were already doing it, now they'll do it more.* Another says: *But men manipulate women, nah. They were already doing it, now they'll do it more.* A fascinatingly thin girl with a green braid hung over one shoulder is leaning by the door and writing in a notebook with a smile on her face. It could be a love poem or it could be maths equations but in either case she is not the kind of woman who will debate the infidelity law. She's a sweet bird of youth, a flower-faced freshness wreathed in green, and looking at her I am struck again by the hominess of this, the intimacy, the ease. I could live here forever, watching the women come and go, noting that flared jeans are in, skinny-fit jeans are in, high-rise jeans are in, long flowery dresses are in, sheath dresses are in, pinafore dresses are in, halterneck tops are in, off-shoulder tops are in, tunic tops are in, platform-heeled sneakers are in, ankle-length boots are in, bathroom slippers are in. Oh the marvellous distraction of clothes and the eternal covetousness for shoes! It joins us together in the Delhi Metro. I like this about women: that looking at each other we become like each other and we masquerade as one. Here there are no battles for space and no need for assertion. We sit squeezed into rows like floppy dolls, and hold out our arms at once if someone misses a step; we make room for the elderly and ill; we help out those weighed down with children or shopping bags.

I remember, suddenly, the obsession my friends and I once developed for a senior in college—just a couple of years older but at that point it felt like an impassable distance, we gawking newbies, she and her gang, experienced sophisticates. A teacher noticed—the giggling and gesturing, the stalking and speculating—and she lit into us one day, outside a classroom, with other students swarming around us, she screamed at us in full public view, and I remember how that wrath passed over everyone and then kept circling back to me. Why did she dislike me? I never understood it till many years later—a grown-up epiphany. It was maybe because she liked me. That mannish jaw, those masculine hands, that awkward imprisonment in a sari. She was expressing longing through tyranny, she was using her authority to harangue us into line when what she desperately wanted was to step out of it herself. I remember thinking then I should find her at once, find some way of apologizing, but I no longer knew where she was, into what thickets of misery that tightly concealed loneliness had led her.

And what would I have said to her? The duality of gender is a giant fiction. We are all bits of everything—androgen, oestrogen, Y chromosome, X chromosome, pink, blue. If we are aggressive then, regardless of gender, we produce the male hormones, say the scientists, and if we are gentle we make female ones. And this too is contingent, for different societies regard different characteristics as male and female. You could be a woman who is also a man and you could be a man who is also a woman. Why this daily battle to keep it all contained within one or the other plotline? There are really five genders, say the scientists, and there could be more to come.

Why am I here then, boxed into the women's compartment of the Delhi Metro as the train pulls into Jor Bagh? Why draw up these rules—on this side of the gangway connection only women, on that side anyone—and then insist they've been there since the world began? To say to oneself—I'm a woman is to also say—be a woman in the prescribed way. Stay safe from men. Call this helpline. Travel in the reserved coach. *Be a woman, be a woman, be a woman.* What if I don't want that tune playing in my head all day? What if I am starting to distrust the idea that women should huddle together, deafen themselves with chants of their vulnerability, veil themselves to emphasize the modesty of their sex, unveil themselves to emphasize the attractiveness of their sex, campaign for the necessity of their difference? What if I want to say to all women: Don't confuse the demand for greater honour and more freedom with the demand for harder boundaries and sharper knives and total exclusivity.

At Green Park I get to sit again and I see a little boy float by—little boys are allowed among the women because the personalities of little boys are more like women's than men's, or because even the powers-that-be agree that it would be cruel to separate little boys from their mothers, or because little boys are children and the category of children has been allowed to override the category of gender. He is holding between his fingers a paper crane, holding it with the delicacy and considering it with the intensity that makes this thing created from a scrap of crinkled peanut-wrapper appear like a work of art. He holds it high and flies it slowly through the compartment but every time he comes too near a passenger's arm or nose or leg, he stops, withdraws shyly, and then starts up his crane again, navigating it carefully again through the throng of female bodies. I wish I could kidnap him when his mother wasn't looking. I wish it turned out he was motherless and destiny had gifted him to me. I wish his paper crane landed on my palm and he said to me—*Yes, you.* If I compiled every child dream I've had I would have made myself an encyclopedia of longing. All the day-time hardening of conviction, all the night-time unravelling with desperation. Where do they come from, these psychic reminders, these atavistic desires? *No, no, no,* I wake up every morning and tell myself. *One is not born, but rather becomes, woman.* And yet some pressing, prehistoric memory keeps resurfacing in the blood, completely out of my reach, laughing at my rationalizations.

Little wandering boy piloting his crane has an older sister who grabs him by the collar and hauls him off the train at Chattarpur. As the doors close, I see his hand still holding the thing aloft to protect it, make sure that any damage his sister inflicts on him does not affect his precious talisman. I try to stop thinking about him and by Sikanderpur I have almost managed to erase him: the little round glasses, the little shoes with Velcro straps, the little pout of seriousness. The warm nasal voice of the announcer is filling my head with warnings: Change here for the . . . Change here for the . . . Change here for a way out of this eternal disjunction. I am nearing the end of the line and beyond that lies the confusing hinterland through which one must make one's way alone. The doors slide open and I get out thinking: I don't know about five genders but maybe there are three—men, women and me.

the origins of origami

JANICE PARIAT

in place of him
a white
bird
a white bird
for remembering.
all hope,
a frozen
landscape,
a sheet
of snow,
a field
vast with latent
loss, she folds
into shape—long
wings, hooded beak,
small claws to perch
on her lonesome
shelf.
as though to say
he must, but this
won't—fly through

an open window, vanish
into the cool, clear
blue of sky.

Who would think it?
this careful, precise
art of giving shape
to emptiness.
only a woman
with no need
for words—hollow,
trite, discarding them
into the night
three centuries
ago, like day's carefully
gathered waste. a swan,

a stork, a flutter of
silent sparrows, each
a brittle memory, a string
of parchment secrets.
in her hands they took
form, a brutal love.
beneath each attentive
fold, razor slivers
of hope.
she used paper
to mould her sadness.

Travelling in the Zone

THE IMAGE IN AN AGE OF BUTTERFLY EFFECTS AND HAYWIRE BOMBS

RANJIT HOSKOTE

Our sense of reality, especially of people, is complex, seldom one-dimensional, and seldom static or fully resolved. The camera, however, is not a mind. It is locked into its single one-point perspective and has no shifting qualitative perceptions. The photograph has no before and after other than what is implied in its single image. It is an exceedingly attenuated version of reality. And that, precisely, is its fascination. It is impossible, I know, but I would like to imbue these pale, two-dimensional rubbings of reality, with their muted tones of grey, not simply with the richness of four-dimensional reality, but also with something of the subtlety and ambiguity of our shifting and frequently contradictory perceptions of reality.

—David Goldblatt, 1998*

All my life, I have been fascinated by the Zone, a devastated area cordoned off from the normality of life in Andrei Tarkovsky's 1979 cinematic masterwork, *Stalker*. An empty district of ruins set at the heart of a shadowy but otherwise functioning region, with roads and railways and timetables, the Zone symbolizes an experience of extinction so complete and so horrible that the authorities have declared it off-limits. Armed border guards forbid visitors entry; the penalty for penetrating the mystery is death. And yet this Zone, haunted and haunting, remains at the centre of life in the misty futuristic scenario that the protagonists of *Stalker* inhabit. So evocative of mortality and apocalypse is this area that, paradoxically, it comes to stand for a temple of enigma where all questions will be answered, all riddles solved.

From time to time, a few determined pilgrims try and enter the prohibited area. They make the perilous journey to the heart of the Zone: an abandoned house where a telephone rings, belling out to fill a solitude as large as the world. Guided by a taciturn, demon-driven man, the eponymous Stalker, these questors have yielded to the Zone's fatal attraction and defied the restrictions of the authorities. What are they: brave men or foolhardy adventurers? Quixotic philosophers or men and women burning with curiosity, demanding answers of the universe? People wishing to bear witness and make their testimony in the face of the unexplained; or votaries of illumination and transformation who come to worship in this strange relic of a battleground where humankind was once tested to the most extreme limits of its endurance?

Today, our normality has been engulfed by the devastation of war, massacre, tyranny and famine. Our lives are dominated by violence and shaped by surveillance: we pass checkpoints without even realising it; cell phone companies rather than watchtower patrols tell us when we have crossed borders. And some borders cannot be passed. They have been lost to clouds rising from explosions, buried under a rain of shrapnel and debris. Cataclysm is everywhere. Wherever we go, we are travelling in the Zone.

II

The contemporary photojournalist is our own Stalker. This is her working context: the Zone as normality, daytime blurring into night-time, the working day hinged by curfew. A hard *k* falls insistently on her ear as she goes about her business: her practice is defined by the leitmotifs of combat, confrontation and catastrophe. She maps the wages of destruction and the arrears of hope.

Of course, the photojournalist has worked at the edge of risk ever since the camera was placed at the service of the headline. When the airship *R-101* exploded, turning into a blazing silk balloon the size of a football field, the photojournalist was there. When Mao struck across the heartland of a continent, driving his treacherous enemies to the edge of the ocean, she was there. When Allied troops threw open the death camps of Birkenau and Bergen Belsen to show the local people the heaped skeletons who survived, she was there. When Jiddu Krishnamurti renounced the claim to the mantle of World Teacher that his devotees had made on his behalf, thus becoming the only modern spiritual teacher to reject the seductions of authority, she was there. When the Berlin Wall came down, bringing a divided people together in an unending night of revelry, she was there. But when unemployment found voice as racist brutality, long after the fallen Wall proved to be a mirage of prosperity, she was there too. And when the US troops staged their spectacles of triumph in Iraq, that was not her most heroic moment: she took orders from the men in uniform, but, here too, she sometimes managed to short-circuit the manual of instructions. Wherever warfare, drought, famine and genocide forced millions of people to migrate across the wastelands of the twentieth century, she was there.

Like the hero of John Steinbeck's *The Grapes of Wrath*, wherever people suffered or drew breath in difficult times, came together in knots of discontent or made their feelings known in protest or riot, the photojournalist was with them. It was her task to slip inside the skin of her subjects, even while maintaining an objective distance: the distance necessary to achieve the accuracy of portraiture, the density of portrayal. The occupational hazards of photojournalism include hairpin bends of fortune and sudden death. This is an art of combat with fate, which has found its natural habitat in chaos, in moments of natural, social or military upheaval.

It is under the banner of Ares/Skanda, the red-eyed god of war, that the camera negotiates the present—whether in high plateaux charted by contending armies or on highways where dawn has claimed an unsuspecting sacrifice, in rooms dank with the smell of terror and suicide, or in the antechambers of intrigue that protect the assemblies of legislation from the anger of the oppressed. At its core, photojournalism speaks of the predicaments of individuals and communities caught up in the churning of the modern world. A world in which, by a butterfly effect, the smallest local event can trigger a global uproar; a minor episode can set off a seismic cascade of upheaval.

And no one is immune. Anyone can be a victim. In a tightly networked world where no man, woman or child is an island entire of itself, disaster is an equal-opportunity phenomenon. The Pentagon's smart bombs can be exceptionally dumb in practice, as we have seen, and their pinpoint perfection can go haywire in free fall. This does not disturb the grand panjandrums of the new empire. All they have to do is issue an official denial and add a statistic or two to the ledgers of damage, collateral or otherwise. And bombs do not simply land behind walls of sandbags in these troubled times. Some of them come hidden in seed bags too, camouflaged as promises of prosperity.

During the last two decades—the opening decades of what was meant to be a new century—we have travelled to Afghanistan, Iraq and Syria through the eyes of photojournalists, and been shattered by the evidence: the lives of individuals and communities lost or brutalized by rapacious contending powers. We have mourned the victims of mass suicides among the farmers of peninsular India, seeing them in illustrated journals as though in reality. Standing at the photojournalist's elbow, we have wept for those who perished in the tsunami that broke over the Indian Ocean littoral; for those who died in the snow tsunami that shattered roofs and buried houses in rural Kashmir; for those blown up by bombs planted in trains in Bombay; and for those who were violated and murdered by the insane absolutisms of Hindutva and jihadism, and by ultra-nationalisms of every shade.

III

Our vocabulary has become warlike even in peacetime. We talk of mission objectives and task forces, even when the furthest we get to the theatre of war is a cricket ground decked with rival colours, or a discreetly panelled boardroom. We talk of buffer zones and safe passages, even in civic discourse concerning sanitation and transport problems. Even the pictures on the sports pages—with goalkeepers crashing in slow motion, hockey sticks raised in salute, athletes gnashing their teeth, and players punching the air —have begun to resemble battlefield images. Television anchors get into flak jackets and strut around their studios, playing out childhood fantasies of being field commanders. All life has become militarized. We are would-be combatants in act and phrase, and this may not be unusual in an epoch when large swathes of the world's land surface are subjected to the strictest controls in the name of martial emergency.

What do the images that appear in newspapers and magazines tell us about ourselves? They are precipitates of our anxieties and aspirations, but mostly of our anxieties. In compressed form, they hold the key narratives of a world produced by technological modernity—which has not become the Utopia of which its progenitors dreamt. Rather, to invoke one of Joseph Conrad's most chilling images, it has revealed itself as the heart of darkness.

I think, specifically, of how my ancestral homeland, Kashmir, is presented through the images of photojournalism today. At their best, these images evoke pity and terror, the classical conditions of tragedy, and force us to ask questions. What is it like to live daily in the shadow of heavy artillery, your identity questioned at every street corner? What is it like to conduct the music of commerce to a score written for a symphony of bazookas and bombs, an orchestra of tanks and snipers? What can childhood mean when its games are played on hillsides planted, not with fruit trees, but with mines? How do individuals cope with a reality that unfolds in the form of bullet-pocked walls and broken windows? Who are these sturdy yet vulnerable figures: this woman walking through a graveyard overcrowded with headstones; this old woman praying under the bayonet; this girl cowering as soldiers ransack her home in search of hidden insurgents?

Through the travelling lens, we dwell on the shadows of suspicion and track the onset of paranoia. We find ourselves moving on a continuous in-and-out spiral between terror and survival, oppression and hope. The key to resolve the manic swing of this spiral is empathy. As the South African photographer David Goldblatt (1930–2018) suggested, in the observation that I have placed at the head of this brief essay, the question before the photojournalist is this: How is the split-second image, taken in the heat of the moment, in real time with a deadline aligned against it, to be charged 'not simply with the richness of four-dimensional reality, but also with something of the subtlety and ambiguity of our shifting and fre-quently contradictory perceptions of reality'? How are the contradictions of being human, the emotional resonances of an encounter with a new or renewed reality, to be encoded into the image registered at speed, in move-ment, on the spur? The picture must be taken in a world where all is in hazard, including your job and your life. And yet, is it too late or too dan-gerous for the picturing Self to reach out to the pictured Other in a gesture of empathy?

In my mind, I picture many hands tearing these images of anguish from magazines and newspapers, and folding them into paper cranes. I picture a flight of paper cranes, thousands of them, gliding across lines of control and no-fly zones, reminding us of a freedom and a joy that were never meant to be divided by boundaries enforced with periodic offerings of blood tribute.

* David Goldblatt, interview with Okwui Enwezor, conducted in Johannesburg, January 1998. See Okwui Enwezor, 'Matter and Consciousness: An Insistent Gaze from a Not Disinterested Photographer' in Corinne Diserens and Okwui Enwezor (eds), *David Goldblatt: Fifty-One Years* (Barcelona: Museu d'Art de Barcelona & Actar, 2001; released on the occasion of a major retrospective of the photographer's work).

The Magic Pants

SHOVON CHOWDHURY

'We need to kill the RSS,' says the Sword of the Lord.

'What, all of them?' I ask.

He has the floor, but I cannot help interjecting. We are at the weekly meeting of the New Delhi Suicide Club. Our members consist of the terminally ill. We have dedicated ourselves to killing all those who have eluded the justice system but deserve to die. We go down, but we take one with us, leaving the world a cleaner place. We spend our meetings identifying targets, and discussing their eligibility, because this is not something that can be done lightly. It requires a process. I helped found this club two years ago. Apparently my diagnosis was premature. I am doing whatever I can in the time I have left. There are so many stories that I could tell you. But let me get on with this one first.

The Sword of the Lord is a Christian gentleman from Kerala, who refuses to tell us his real name. 'I am the Sword of the Lord,' he said, on arrival, 'and I have found you!' He is bearded, gaunt and wild-eyed. He is in the early stages of leukaemia. He nurses many grudges.

'RSS is like a cancer on the nation!' he says, pounding the arm of my sofa. 'They must be eradicated fully!'

I am afraid to delve any deeper. I hope he hasn't worked out a plan. The insanity does not bother me. All of us here have been driven mad, to a greater or lesser extent, by injustices. But our actions need to be well planned, and carefully thought through. This is where my diplomatic skills come in. That's why they made me the secretary. I may be homicidal, but otherwise, I'm well balanced.

'I'll tell you what,' I say, 'let me visit one of their branches on a fact-finding mission. I'll make friends with them, and lull them into a false sense of security. Once we know them better, we can formulate a plan of action.'

Of course, we won't do anything of the sort. His scheme is impractical. There are far too many of them. I'll just visit a few times until the Sword of the Lord starts obsessing about something else. But I should go there with some kind of objective in mind. It seems such a waste otherwise. Now that my time is limited, I feel the need to be useful.

Becoming an RSS member is easy. All I have to do is apply online and wait for a call. Their customer service is quite good. I receive a call in less than an hour from Mishra-ji, the local boss. I am honoured that the boss is calling personally, and tell him so. 'Beginning is the most important part of any process,' says Mishra-ji. 'If bad elements get into the organization, we will be weakened. That's why I attend the first call personally. First of all please tell me, are you a man or a woman?'

I am surprised. I have always been proud of my voice, which is deep and manly. It goes with my moustache. People often compliment me. I confirm that I am male. 'No offence, I have to check. We do not allow women to join. Sometimes they try to fool me by deepening their voices on the phone.' I assure him that this is not so.

'What language do you prefer to speak in? I noticed that your name is Bengali.' I am proud of my hard-earned Hindi skills. This is a chance to demonstrate. I speak at length about my passion for Hindus, and how all the injustices against them makes my blood boil. I sneer at the politics of appeasement. I make it clear that while I would normally never support violence, there are times when a man has to do what a man has to do, in order to preserve our greatness.

He listens carefully. 'In the beginning, it's best if you speak less,' he says. 'Come and join us at the Saraswati Shishu Mandir playground at 6.30 a.m. tomorrow.' He disconnects before I can say 'Jai Hind!' I'm a little upset. I've been practising.

That evening I stand in front of the mirror. This is the moment of truth. Can I go out in public dressed like this? The white shirt is fine, and even the black cap will do. Someone once told me that the black represents evil, but it's the khakis that are the problem. They are short and wide and billowy, cut off above the knee. I look like a ballerina affiliated to the armed forces. I will have to walk all the way to the playground, in public, wearing them. I stand there for a long time, unable to look away. I pull in my stomach, but the shape of the pants does not change. No wonder people wearing these pants are angry, especially when they get older, and have been wearing them for years. Who can blame them? The things they must have gone through; the taunts and embarrassment. I will myself to conquer my fears. I fill myself with steely resolve. If I want to infiltrate their ranks, these pants are unavoidable.

It's hard work being in the RSS. I had to get up at five. We salute the orange flag, sing a song and do some yoga. Then it's time for stick drill. There are no generational biases here. All ages are welcome, so long as they are male. There are senior citizens and boys as young as seven or eight, whirling their sticks and striking poses. The sticks are heavy. 'When do we get to use them?' I ask Chandidas, one of my new friends. He pokes Govardhan, another new friend, in the ribs, and laughs. 'See this one, he's full of energy!'

After a brief speech from Mishra-ji on cow-urine therapy, I join Chandidas, Govardhan and Johnny at a nearby teashop. I eye the tea boy suspiciously. 'He looks like a Muslim,' I tell Chandidas. I assume this is the kind of thing they discuss.

Chandidas shakes his head. He is in his thirties, apple-cheeked and bespectacled. He looks like a junior bank officer, which is what he is. 'He's a child, let him be. I know you want to fit in, brother, but it's OK. We're not like that. We have differences with Muslims on policy and philosophy, but we do not hate them personally.'

'Actually I do hate them, a little bit,' says Govardhan. 'Me too,' says Johnny. 'They are intent on eating our mother. As if no other food is available.' Johnny is the third member of the group, thin, dark and extremely pessimistic. He delivers food for a popular food app, which is how he met Govardhan, who runs a small restaurant. Of the three, he seems the most reasonable.

Isn't Johnny a slightly strange name for a Hindu warrior, I ask him, when we first met. 'It's OK,' says Govardhan, 'We have to be tolerant. Why get upset about small-small things?' We discuss the state of the nation over several cups of tea. They appear to be angry. They nurse many resentments. Eventually, I leave, saying I have to go to office. This is not true. I resigned months ago, in order to cleanse the country.

They meet every morning, every single day. I am in awe of their discipline. Many of my friends are communists, but the communists don't stand a chance. They never do any group activities, except drinking rum. Over the course of the next week, I become physically fitter. My cheeks begin to glow. I almost forget about the pants I have to wear.

I feel the confidence to ask probing questions, so that I can understand them better. 'Please don't mind, Mishra-ji,' I ask him one day before dispersal, 'But what about Gandhi-ji? People say that Godse, his killer, was an RSS man?' To my surprise, Mishra-ji is quite pleased by my question.

'Many people ask me this,' he says, 'It's a popular misconception. This is why all history books need to be rewritten, so that the right things are brought out properly. Did you know that we were investigated for twenty-two years in the matter of Gandhi's death? Still they couldn't find anything, and they had to publish the report in 1970, saying the RSS as such was not responsible. Others say obviously we are guilty, because our founder was a devotee of Savarkar-ji, and Godse-ji was also a devotee of Savarkar-ji. What kind of logic is this? Take the case of renowned cine star Amitabh-ji. Are all followers of Amitabh-ji the same? If one of them commits a crime, are all of them guilty? It's very wrong to generalize about an entire community like that.'

Today's discussion was cut short. A Hindu procession was passing by a mosque. They all rushed off to make sure it passed unhindered.

A theory has begun to form in my mind. I decide to start testing it the next day when it's my turn to practice public speaking. 'This is a forum for debate and discussion,' I say. 'Instead of giving a lecture, I want to ask a question. Why don't we allow women to join us?'

I can see that quite a few of the others want to know this too. They clasp and unclasp their sticks nervously as Mishra-ji gets up. He gestures for me to sit down. 'Sometimes new people come in with new ideas. We always welcome them. But there are reasons for everything. This is a question that some of you have previously raised from time to time. You have even provided examples. Delhi Public School is a very successful institution, you have pointed out, despite being co-educational. It, too, is spreading rapidly across the country. In Gurugram alone, there are six of them. But they are a product of Western thought process. In our own culture and tradition, women have a different role. The Rashtra Sevika Samiti is there for their upliftment. It is foolish to ask why women are not here. If you went to a men's hockey match, would you ask, where are the women? No. For that, you have to see a women's hockey match. In any case, it is not that we are completely cut off from them. I myself go to the Badarpur shakha of the Sevika Samiti once a month, to supervise their activities. Once you reach my level, after twenty to thirty years, you too will be able to visit them.'

The group disperses sadly, heads down, shuffling their feet. 'But by then, it will be too late,' whispers Johnny, morosely.

Our session at the teashop is gloomy. I try to cheer them up by assuring them that the Ram Temple at Ayodhya is bound to be built soon, but this fails to elicit much enthusiasm. 'They will never build it,' says

Chandidas, munching disconsolately on a Marie biscuit. 'Once the temple is built, what will they talk about during elections?' He offers Johnny a biscuit. Johnny declines, politely. 'I'm not hungry,' he says. 'I had a lot of deliveries last night. I stopped on the way and ate Kung Pao Paneer, Vegetable Chop Suey, and three kinds of vegetable fried rice, and washed it down with gulab jamun syrup. I eat about twenty per cent of each dish. Restaurants nowadays provide utensils; it's become very easy. I just open the containers and re-seal them after eating. It's all very hygienic, except for the gulab jamuns. Those I have to squeeze with my fingers.'

He notices my expression. 'Don't you judge me!' he snarls. 'At least I'm not putting my dick in the pasta. Several of my colleagues do that for fun. One of them was even hospitalized with second-degree burns.'

I am never ordering food online again.

The next morning, I steer the conversation towards women once more. I am looking for a life partner, I say. Now that I have made these new connections, is there any way in which they can guide me? Govardhan sighs deeply. 'You have come to the wrong place, brother. I have been married for fourteen years. So many times, I have tried to indulge in an extramarital affair, but other women are not willing to entertain me.' 'I am facing the same problem,' says Chandidas. 'I think they find me funny. They prefer all those fancy-speaking leftist types.' He grinds his teeth. Johnny looks down at the floor, moodily. It's fair to assume that he's not getting lucky either.

I look at them, sitting there, lacking love, their khaki pants limp and gaping. It comes to me in a flash. I know exactly what to do. It will take me around a week to sort out, I reckon. I get up briskly. 'Next week, then?' I say, trying to convey with my tone how next week will be special. They nod limply. I leave with a spring in my step, secure in the knowledge of how much happiness I am going to bring. This is a whole new approach for me. I am going to ensure justice without murdering anyone.

For the first two days, I google pants. The alpine hiking pants look good. So do the waterproof surfer pants. I consider something in denim. They might even go for the distressed look. It's not that unfamiliar. Priyanka Chopra is rocking it constantly. But then I decide not to push it. What I need is something in a durable fabric that hangs well and moulds the butt discreetly. Finally, on a Chinese website, I find the perfect pair. I order a dozen.

When I make my pitch to the boys, I hold the pants up and flap them a little. 'Genuine Japanese technology! Waterproof! Fireproof!' These pants have many qualities, but I've decided to lead with the technology angle. I'm lying about the fireproofing. They're highly inflammable, but this is a good thing. The boys seem mostly harmless, but in case they start setting fire to anything, they will be the first ones to burn. 'As a successful exporter, I spent many years in Japan cultivating relationships,' I tell them. 'That's how I can get such a good price for you. See, I became so close to them, they even taught me to do this. It's a secret they don't share with everyone.' I pull out a small piece of paper and make them a paper crane. 'This is also Japanese, they call it origami.' They pass the crane around. It's a little thing of wonder. Their spirits lighten in front of my eyes. I tell them what they have to do.

'It's very simple,' I say. 'Wear these pants. Go to any Udupi or other pure vegetarian restaurant. If you see a lady you like, try to sit at a table next to her. Don't be shy. One of the other plus points of these pants is that your butt will look magnificent. That's half the battle. Then you take a small piece of paper and turn it into a paper crane. Do it slowly, so that she can see you doing it. Linger over every fold. Once you finish, you can drop it on her table, as if by mistake, and excuse yourself while you pick it up. I can guarantee you, a conversation will start. Women like men to be interesting. A paper crane from Japan makes you interesting. If you also know how to read palms, the matter is practically settled.'

They are more enthusiastic than I have ever seen them before. Their hearts are filled with hope. I take out the pants and throw a couple to each of them, making broad estimations regarding size. 'Now go forwards, my friends, and fly! I'll come back in a week and check on your progress.'

I know I may not live long, but I've decided to convert my RSS activities to a weekly cycle. Five in the morning is way too early.

From the moment they see me, they can barely suppress their excitement. They fidget through the morning session. Afterwards, in the teashop, they envelop me in a group hug. 'Three times!' says Govardhan, 'Three times in one day!' 'Really?' I ask, impressed by his stamina. 'Yes!' says Govardhan, 'three times I talked to her. Three separate sentences she spoke to me. It was wonderful!' 'I also succeeded,' says Chandidas. 'She asked me to make her another one.' 'Afterwards, we shared half a plate of Gobi Manchurian,' says Johnny, 'she asked to keep the plastic fork, and I let her!'

They babble excitedly, sharing their experiences. They are vastly different from the angry, sad men I have known this past month. They are filled with positive energy. 'Now all you have to do is convince Mishra-ji to take this as our uniform,' they say. 'We will all be right behind you. We will give you our full support.'

When I actually meet him, they stand very quietly, behind a few of the others. Mishra-ji is dubious. 'Mishra-ji, you are always emphasising the need for debate and discussion,' I say. 'Shouldn't every proposal receive a fair trial? Do one thing. Wear one pair of these pants at your next meeting of the Sevika Samiti.' After some hesitation, Mishra-ji agrees. I hand over a pair in size XXL, hoping for the best.

'One of them pinched my butt,' whispers Mishra-ji as we salute the orange flag the following week. He is just back from a meeting with the Sevika Samiti, where he delivered a brief lecture on paneer. His expression is awestruck. His cheeks are glowing. 'Then I have a statement to make during Public Speaking,' I whisper back.

I stand to attention, next to the flag, tall and proud, holding up the pants for everyone to see. 'Mishra-ji, I formally request you to accept these pants as official wear for this shakha. All members will bear their own expenses. Mishra-ji, I know you value tradition, but these pants are not very different. They are also khaki coloured. Shape is very similar. Not to mention fireproof. The netting inside means no underwear is required. They have more pockets. They are a miracle of Japanese design.' Mishra-ji looks hesitant. But I can see that he is tempted. 'Swami Vivekananda was a big admirer of the Japanese. He kept telling the Indian youth, get up off your backsides, be more like the Japanese! In a way, you will be honouring him.'

Mishra-ji smiles. The gathering erupts in cheers. I bring out my small notepad and start taking down orders.

That went well. I feel quite pleased. One shakha down, 99,986 to go. I am optimistic. The word will spread. Demand will rise. Wherever it reaches, my pants and I will be there, along with our flying cranes.

Cranes in Persian, or Urdu

GOPIKA JADEJA

The learned Šahmardān b. Abi'l-Ḳayr, in his *Nozhat-nāma-ye ʿalā'ī* (*c.* 490-95 / 1097-1102; p. 136), described the migrating pattern of cranes, which fly in large numbers and in single file. Each flock is led by one bird, which at intervals is outdistanced and replaced by the bird immediately following, so that each bird in the file 'might enjoy the honor and prestige of leadership'. When the flocks rest at night, always far from people and such predators as foxes and jackals, the birds take turns keeping watch, and the watching bird stands on one leg in order not to fall asleep.

—Hušang Aʿlam, 'Crane'*

When you imagined them, the cranes did not make their whoops in a language I know. Neither Persian nor Urdu. My tongue mimics the sonic shapes of Devanagari, the troughs and crests of a script that flows like water, a language I have lost.

I never heard it from you, but it was always your voice when mother recited it, my first lesson in exile and loss, the poem about migratory cranes returning home. Your cadence punctuated the sound of the arrow that found the wing of the saras; it's fall, slow motion, to earth.

A first lesson in violence, the lines describing the hunter and the hunted. Smell of blood and love as the saras fell, its mate hovering above. No possibility of a return home. The flock paused mid-flight, home written on wings. The air aflutter before the rush of wings fleeing arrows.

Like you, I borrow words. Make them speak in a different tongue. Yet I cannot translate into words the wounds and the wounded. Maybe it needs no translation. In your voice, my mother reciting through her tears, I see that you knew the wound is the place the light enters you.

* Hušang A'lam, 'Crane' in *Encyclopædia Iranica*, online edition, 2018. Available at: http://bit.ly/2rRQdUz (last accessed 12 December 2019).

Aziz from Pakistan

SAMRAT CHOUDHURY

I bumped into Aziz at Tokyo's Narita Airport. We had coincidentally arrived on the same connecting flight from Bangkok and were at the same counter to change money. He was in front of me, a fair-skinned man with brown hair. I took him to be East European. Later, he was in front of me again when I reached the information desk near the exit to figure out which bus I needed to take into town. I noticed we were holding identical printouts of the same map.

'Excuse me,' I asked, 'are you going to the International House of Japan?'

He was.

We introduced ourselves. Samrat, from India. And Aziz, from Pakistan.

We realized we were both in Japan for the same fellowship, the Asian Leadership Fellows Program. At IHJ, we wound up staying in adjacent rooms. It so happened that we were also the only two smokers among the fellows. Naturally, we ended up hanging out together quite often.

Aziz had studied philosophy at college in London and had something of the distracted air of the philosopher. He also had a considerable memory for Urdu couplets and jokes. Conversations with him were fun, ranging from the ruminative to the poetic. There was only one topic I think we tip-toed around, at least initially: politics.

Aziz is from the mountainous Gilgit-Baltistan region of Pakistan. It is an area that inhabits a curious space between multiple powers. There were independent principalities in Gilgit-Baltistan till 1974, but since then the region has been embroiled in the Kashmir dispute, the festering heart of a seemingly endless rivalry between India and Pakistan. On Indian maps, the area appears as the northernmost part of Jammu and Kashmir. Moreover, it has the Chinese province of Xinjiang as a neighbour. China's Belt and Road Initiative cuts through it.

I come from Meghalaya in the hills of Northeast India. Ethnically, I am Bengali; my ancestors lost their lands and homes in the Partition of India when the country was divided along religious lines into Hindu-majority India and Muslim-majority Pakistan. Some relatives, who remained in what became East Pakistan in 1947, escaped with their lives—and barely anything else—when the Pakistan Army began the genocide of 1971 that led to war with India and the creation of Bangladesh. Those events still live on in today's contentious politics of citizenship in India.

Relations between Aziz's country and mine have been fraught since the start. In 1947, there were the horrific communal riots in which an esti-mated million people died. There was also the first, limited war between the two countries that left the state of Jammu and Kashmir unhappily divided between India and Pakistan. Two more wars followed, in 1965 and 1971. A third conflict broke out in 1999. The previous year, 1998, both countries had conducted nuclear tests.

Two years later, in 2001, the situation again became very tense after India's parliament was attacked by terrorists who Indian security agencies believed were from the Jaish-e-Mohammad and Lashkar-e-Tayyeba, both Muslim fundamentalist outfits with bases in Pakistan. Then, in 2008, there was another major terrorist attack, this time on the city of Mumbai. A Pakistani terrorist of the Lashkar-e-Tayyeba, Ajmal Kasab, was caught alive.

These days, there is a state of permanent hostility between the countries, at least in the media, if not on the border. I have largely stopped watching television news because the endless, screaming sensationalism, on practically every topic, is more akin to reality TV than news, and the hysteria reaches its pinnacle when the topic is Pakistan.

While I have not been to Pakistan, nor watched Pakistani news television, Aziz said the tone there towards India is not very different.

Keeping off TV, however, is not enough to escape the endless stream of chest-thumping nationalism that pervades our other media: on Twitter, and on my mobile phone, uninvited, via some WhatsApp group or other. Every day brings fresh posts either about the endless perfidies of Pakistan, or the greatness of our soldiers. Terrorists, 'anti-nationals'—meaning anyone considered insufficiently patriotic by the flag-waving standards of self-appointed nationalists, and Muslims—usually long-dead rulers of medieval kingdoms located in the Indian subcontinent, are other frequent subjects of angry posts and news reports.

Kashmir is the focus and subject of much nationalism on both sides of the border. I wondered what Aziz, whom I had assumed initially was Kashmiri, thought of the whole situation from the other side, but it seemed a difficult topic to broach early on in our acquaintanceship. However, after a few days, I discovered that he is not a Kashmiri at all. He is a Shina speaker—a member of an ethnic community whose existence I had been unaware of until I met Aziz. It further emerged that there is considerable diversity of language and ethnicity in his part of the world, just as there is in mine; Kashmiris are merely one among many communities in what appears on Indian maps as Jammu and Kashmir. Moreover, Aziz personally was less than happy to have Gilgit-Baltistan dragged into the interregional conflict. As a Shina and a Pakistani, he opposed what he called 'Kashmiri colonialism', asserting that his province shared no common history, language or culture with the dominant community of the area.

He showed me pictures of his home. It is a beautiful place, with snow-capped mountains and glades. I saw pictures of his children: sweet, smiling kids. In turn, I pulled out some pictures of my own: of the rolling green hills and Shire-like landscapes of Meghalaya.

Identity is complicated. I was born and brought up in Meghalaya. I left after graduating from high school, only to return twenty-four years later in 2017. But I still don't know if I belong there. I am, after all, a descendant of refugees. A Bengali—prone to easy labelling as a Bangladeshi anywhere in Northeast India, a region that has seen waves of ethnic cleansing directed against local ethnic minorities, both Hindu and Muslim. Currently, an ongoing exercise to draw up a National Register of Citizens in the state of Assam has excluded 1.9 million people, around 1.5 million of them believed to be Hindu and Muslim Bengalis, from the list. India's current home minister, Amit Shah, has promised to extend this exercise to the entire country.

I realized that Aziz, in a different way, was also part of a sometimes-persecuted minority in his country. He was an Ismaili, a denomination of Islam that has come under attack by fundamentalists in Pakistan.

Our stories didn't fit the standard narratives that played out every day in our countries. We were Indian and Pakistani, Hindu and Muslim, but we existed in liminal spaces.

One evening, when out for our usual smoke, I awkwardly brought up the day's news. Indian forces had shot at a helicopter carrying the prime minister of what Pakistan calls 'Azad Kashmir' and India refers to 'Pakistan-Occupied Kashmir'. While the Indian Army said the helicopter had violated Indian airspace across the Line of Control, the de facto border between the two sides, the prime minister of Azad Kashmir denied that such a breach had taken place. Aziz muttered something about how this sort of nonsense kept happening, and we went on to talk about concerns closer to us at the moment, such as planning a trip out of Tokyo. The first place we decided to go to was Hiroshima.

Everything in Japan works like clockwork; quiet clockwork. Even busy train stations are surprisingly noiseless and orderly. People taking the Shinkansen bullet train line up directly in front of the spot where their coach will pull up, at exactly the appointed minute. They board the train silently and efficiently. The train departs a minute or two later, as scheduled.

So much timeliness and orderliness are hard for Indians and Pakistanis alike. Fortunately, we had already been in the country for a month and though we continued to marvel at the punctuality, cleanliness and quietness of public services, we were also mentally prepared for it. The two of us, along with a Malaysian colleague, reached the train station well before our departure time, lined up at the exact spot where the coach would stop, and boarded silently, even managing to stow our bags without fuss.

The journey was fast and uneventful, as is the Japanese norm. The train arrived in Hiroshima, 800 km away, at exactly the scheduled hour and minute. We disembarked quietly, efficiently and swiftly. After this proud achievement, we further distinguished ourselves by silently and efficiently taking one of the silent and efficient streetcars that ply from just outside the train station.

The neat little apartment that we had booked on the Airbnb app was close to the Atomic Bomb Dome. It was a grey morning, with a typhoon approaching, when we walked across a bridge to the Dome. It is one of two buildings near the Hypocentre, the exact spot over which the 15-kiloton atom bomb was dropped on 6 August 1945, that remained standing after the explosion. An estimated 146,000 men, women and children died because of the bomb. Not all the deaths were instantaneous; tens of thousands died slow, painful deaths from cancer, years after the attack.

Crowds thronged the area. Many, like us, appeared to be foreigners. People did the usual touristy things, taking photos and selfies. Aziz, who likes pictures of himself, posed for a few that I clicked for him. He returned the favour. We took a selfie together with the Dome in the background. We were both aware of the irony of a Pakistani and an Indian, citizens of hostile nuclear neighbours, taking a selfie with the Atomic Bomb Dome in the background.

The river Ota flows past the Dome and through the Peace Park that surrounds it. There is an open-air cafe on the riverside near a little jetty from where boats for the island of Miyajima depart. Gusty winds, early indicators of an approaching storm, knocked over a large garbage bin in the cafe. A Caucasian woman with an American accent rushed to pick up the trash that spilled out. The waitresses, two young locals, raced in to take over the task, thanking her profusely. Aziz and I had stepped up to lend a hand if required, but there was no need. We went off to explore the Peace Park.

Close to the Dome we came across a statue of a woman's figure holding a bunch of flowers. All around it, streamers of colourful origami paper cranes dangled. A little girl posed happily for a photograph, strings of colourful cranes swaying behind her.

Across the Motoyasu bridge over the river ('about 130 metres from the hypocentre' according to a plaque) we came to a large bell that the stormy wind was ringing. Atop it stood a statue of a girl holding a metal shaped in the form of an origami paper crane in her outstretched hands. It was the Children's Peace Monument, a memorial inspired by the death of Sadako Sasaki, a child who was two years old when the bomb fell on Hiroshima. She was blown out of the house by the blast but survived with no apparent damage, until more than nine years later when she came down with leukaemia, slowly wasting away to a painful death over the next eleven months. During her illness, her father told her the story of the thousand paper cranes—an old belief in Japanese culture that anyone who folded a thousand origami paper cranes would be granted their wish. Sadako tried to do so, because she wished to live, but it was not to be.

A museum that commemorates victims of the nuclear holocaust was next. At the centre of it was a dome-shaped hall plastered with the image of Hiroshima right after the bombing. It was a picture of sheer devastation. The hall was empty save for a waterbody in the middle where a woman with the Star of David on her bag stood praying silently, her two little children by her side. The next room had the names and faces of those who had died in the bombing.

Later, we watched short video stories of some of the dead. There was, for instance, the schoolboy aged thirteen from the outskirts of Hiroshima who had been unwell but chose to go to school in the town that fateful day. His mother saw the mushroom cloud and waited in vain for his return. He was eventually brought back, wounded but alive, but his wounds would not stop bleeding. His condition continued to worsen until, after a couple of weeks, he died.

There was a visitor book near the exit. I wrote down my hope for the world, that it should never see such horrors again. Aziz was waiting behind me to write his bit. I knew, without needing to ask, that he wrote of peace.

That evening we finally had a proper chat about our two countries and the difficult history between them; about where it all began, with Partition. For our countries there had been no catharsis. There were no shared museums or memorials that remembered the many ordinary people, Hindus, Muslims, Sikhs and others, who lost their lives in the collective madness that gripped the country in the throes of separation. There was nothing to help us reflect on the Bangladesh genocide and the 1971 war, on Kashmir and the endless sabre-rattling by hawks on both sides, on Northeast India and its own separatist conflicts, on the status of minorities in our own countries. We shared a history and a subcontinent but we did not share, in any reflective way, our thoughts and memories.

India is a country of around 780 spoken languages, and holds within its borders adherents of every major world religion and sizable populations of various racial groups. The nineteenth-century European notion that only people with a common language, religion or ethnicity must belong to one nation is absurd to any Indian who pauses to think about his country. This is true for Pakistan as well. It may be less diverse than India, but it nonetheless—despite the homogenizing efforts of its fundamentalists— has a considerable plurality of languages, ethnicities and cultures. However, its refusal to give political and cultural space and recognition to its eastern territories led to its dismemberment and the creation of Bangladesh. It remains troubled by the fundamentalist quest for purity—a quest now increasingly mirrored, in matters ranging from citizenship registers to the violent enforcement of food taboos, in India.

Through much of history, for thousands of years, linguistic and ethnic nationalisms were unknown to the world, including the Indian subcontinent. Large parts of it were effectively nonstate spaces. When states, in the form of kingdoms, did exist, they were almost inevitably multi-ethnic. Identities and boundaries were fluid. Lives were lived locally, under local chieftains. We have forgotten the newness of our imagined identities, and the nationalisms that go with them.

According to the official map of India, Aziz is an Indian, because Gilgit-Baltistan appears as part of Jammu and Kashmir. It is likely however, that the majority of even the most nationalistic Indians would fail to actually pinpoint Gilgit on a map. The same might very well be true of nationalistic Pakistanis looking at maps of Kashmir.

Nationalists seem to like maps that show large territories as belonging to their countries. It's almost as though they believe that makes them proxy landlords, owners of all that land.

What did the Japanese people gain from Japan's early twentieth-century attempts to become a colonial power, to own maps with large territories? Was the brief pleasure of looking at large swathes of territory on maps worth the Second World War? Post-war Japan rapidly became a First World country—a feat that clearly did not require the possession of colonies. The people grew prosperous, and now live, on average, the longest lives of any nationality on earth. The country as a whole is advanced. By this, I do not only mean the existence of robots and bullet trains but even the small, commonplace things that both Aziz and I, Pakistani and Indian, kept marvelling at. For instance, we were both impressed, even astonished, by how clean the whole country was. 'Shoes get cleaner by walking on the roads here,' Aziz joked. 'The underside of my shoe is sparkling,' I wisecracked. But we were only telling the truth.

We were amazed that even young children in school uniforms took the metro by themselves. There are probably dodgy spots somewhere in the country, and there are occasional crimes, but on the whole, it seemed a very safe place. Once, an American professor who lives in Tokyo told me about the time he had lost his wallet in a bar in the neighbourhood of Roppongi, famous for its nightclubs. He told the bartender, who asked him to wait. He is not sure how, but the wallet was returned to him with more money than it had originally! A Chinese colleague of ours left her laptop on a train. She called the rail company to report it. Her laptop was found and couriered back to her within twenty-four hours.

Aziz and I both told each other that we were becoming more Japanese by the day. We waited patiently for traffic lights to turn green even on empty side streets before walking across. We spoke softly. We queued up for everything. We took for granted that no one would try to rob or cheat us. We expected everything to work as it was supposed to and for everyone to do what they said they would. We were, in other words, becoming quite unsuited to life in the cities of our home countries.

People say all kinds of things about progress. To me, the development indices that mark progress are quite easy to spot. I know I am in an advanced society when people can safely drink the tap water and walk the streets confident in the knowledge that they will not be run over, robbed or molested. A far cry from the India of today.

People say all kinds of things about peace. But, peace is not the mere absence of war. It is that, of course, but it is also the smaller things: the peace in our homes, neighbourhoods and cities, and in the ordinariness of our daily lives, that comes from trust in our fellow citizens.

I thought of the American woman, rushing to pick up the trash that had spilled at the cafe near the Atomic Bomb Dome in Hiroshima, a spot that had been reduced to radioactive rubble by the actions of her country. I thought of the woman with the Star of David on her bag, probably Jewish, praying with her children at the memorial for victims of a different holocaust. I thought of Aziz, my newfound Pakistani friend, insisting on carrying my little backpack for hours when my neck was hurting.

Compassion and kindness are inherently human traits. The children from around the world who send a steady stream of origami cranes, millions of them, with their wishes of peace year after year, are just ordinary kids being kids. The astonishing thing about war in today's world is that it happens at all. No normal person would wish it on any of the world's peoples. They would wish one another peace, in their homes, neighbourhoods, cities and hearts.

The Maid

VEENA VENUGOPAL

It all started with the oversize glasses her son had found downstairs: bright blue, with an exaggerated cats' eye that ended in golden tips. She had asked him to throw them away. But when Sonia Sarm opened her drawer full of sunglasses the following afternoon, there it was. The servant! She must have put them there. 'Mili, Mili, idhar aao,' she yelled. Mili appeared, a broom in one hand, wiping her forehead with the other. 'Why have you kept this here?' Sonia snapped. Mili stepped forwards to see the offending item. 'It was on the table, Didi, so I thought it was yours,' she said.

Sonia rolled her eyes. Really, how could Mili ever think she would wear something as garish as this? 'It's garbage. Rishi picked it up from somewhere. Throw it away,' she said. Mili took it and walked away. A minute later, when Sonia followed her into the kitchen, she found her standing there, the glasses on her face, trying to glimpse her reflection on the polished surface of the cupboards. She looked ridiculous, like a dog on a skateboard. 'Hold it,' Sonia said. She came back with her phone, turned Mili to the light, and quickly took a picture.

Back in the living room, Sonia laboured over the caption. 'My servant's idea of coolness,' she typed. In the ladies' Facebook group that she was a part of there had lately been some policing of language. She remembered someone being shredded apart in the comments for referring to her 'servant'. So what should she say instead? Maid? She googled. 'Is maid OK for servant?' but the results weren't relevant to her research. This was too much work for the phone.

She opened her laptop and after a long search found the offending post on the group that had led to the dissection of the semantics of the word 'servant'. 'Maid', it seems, was OK but not ideal. 'Household help' was more acceptable, but to Sonia it seemed to lack a spark, more like a term from a government file. Finally, she returned to her phone, and uploaded the photo. 'My home manager', she wrote, expecting a few laughs at the exaggeration of the job title, as well as the glasses Mili was wearing.

The likes started pouring in almost immediately. The group had some six thousand members, so anything less than a hundred likes indicated the post had fallen flat. Sonia watched as the number crawled up. After ten minutes or so, the first comment rolled in. 'She looks really cool with them.' And then that comment started getting liked. This, Sonia hadn't expected. 'Agree,' someone said. 'I like the way she's not smiling in the picture, almost looks like Meryl Streep from *The Devil Wears Prada*.' Sonia struggled to figure out what was going on? Were they joking or was all of this serious? She waited an hour. Mili finished her work and left. Another hour later Rishi came home from school. Later, Mili returned to knead the dough and make chapattis for dinner. And all this while, the likes and the comments grew. They seemed to hail Mili as some kind of fashion icon. By about eleven, when the family had gone to bed, Sonia read through the messages again, carefully parsing them for sarcasm. She couldn't find any. She took a deep breath, and then finally wrote: 'When I saw these glasses at the store, I knew they would be perfect for Mili. Even though they were branded and quite expensive, I decided to buy them as a gift for her. We are both thrilled.' With a quivering thumb, she pressed the button that said 'Post'.

The next morning, the post had garnered over 800 likes. Her comment was liked by 357 people. A string of praises called her a marvellous employer, a good person. The hashtag #StayBlessed appeared more than a hundred times.

Confusing as all this was, Sonia was thrilled. For months before this, Sonia had tried all kinds of things to get some traction on the group. First, she had delinked her personal account from it, so that she could change her name. It was ridiculous to imagine there was anything glamorous at all about her real name, Sonu Sharma. She considered Sonia Sharma, it would be easy to explain away Sonu as a pet name. The Sharma was a bigger problem, utterly common, as it could be anyone from a milkman to a godman. After casting around for days, she eventually settled on Sarm. When she first began posting in the group, there were some questions about her unusual surname. 'Long story,' she would reply, punctuated with an eyeroll emoji, but offered no other explanation.

She tried to start discussions on TV shows, she uploaded make-up videos—adjusting her persona from 'expert' to 'cute'—and kept a record of the number of likes garnered. She rarely went over 200. She posted pictures of Rishi when he was a baby, she tried to bake a cake, she danced to a popular song. Nothing seemed to work. She copied a poem about motherhood from somewhere on the internet and posted it as her own. At 280 likes, that had been her biggest hit so far.

The group was full of perfect women preening and primping. The sari tutors had a great following, a genre that was so successful that there wasn't room for any more entries. The DIY divas too had risen rapidly. It was virtually impossible to find a niche in the group. And when you did, it took everything to hold on to it. Why, even the cancer survivors barely got more than a hundred likes these days, no matter how many bald-headed photos they posted.

The success of Mili should have made Sonia happy. Instead she found herself confused. She read and reread the comments, slowly, willing the hidden message to reveal itself. There seemed to be none. They appeared genuinely pleased about how Sonia treated Mili. And so, she let a week pass.

The following Thursday, which she regarded as a high-traffic day, she ordered some biryani at lunchtime. When it arrived, she unboxed her best crockery. She packed the biryani tightly in a bowl and upended it carefully on the white ceramic plate with golden flowers. She removed the errant grains of rice, so the food stayed in a perfect yellow dome, and then with a spoon carefully drew two concentric circles around it; the first, with the gravy that came with the biryani, and then the raita. She did the same on another plate with the remaining rice, and on this she made two bold swipes of the gravy and raita. She assessed the plates, her eyes darting from one to the other. She photographed them, separately, then jointly. After an hour of trying various lighting and filters, finally she uploaded the best photo of the plate. 'Mili watched Masterchef with me yesterday, and this is my lunch today,' she wrote. Sonia found herself holding her breath, but within seconds the ping-ping-ping of the notifications began. 'Awsum', 'you're so lucky', 'east or west, Mili is the best': the comments crowded in. In all, some 700 likes before she turned in for the night, and more than 200 comments.

Careful not to overdo it, from then on, once a week Sonia would put up a Mili-related post: 'I am looking for a sari for Mili. She wants blue and gold'; 'Is there a good doctor you recommend for skin issues? I want to make sure Mili's mole checks out'; 'Mili brought us some special kheer she made at home. Please excuse the dented steel bowl she packed it in'; 'Exhausted. Just back from driving Mili to the railway station, she is going to her village for a fortnight'; 'My son learnt to make origami cranes in school. Look at all our attempts. Of course, the best cranes are Mili's.'

Sonia luxuriated in the comments. People admired her for how well she looked after Mili. 'No one would do the things for their maids that you do for Mili,' one wrote. Everyone agreed. 'Girls please don't call them "maids",' Sonia corrected. 'She is my Home Manager.'

Sonia crafted her strategy for her Mili posts, so they wouldn't seem inauthentic. Praise, followed by concern, with a couple of jokes thrown in seemed to be the best formula. She worked hard, teaching Mili a few words in English, then posting a video of her attempts. 'I love my country, but for people like Mili English is their ticket out of poverty,' she wrote. Applause! She bought cheap fabric from stores, cutting them up in squares and triangles: 'Teaching Mili some tailoring skills.' Louder applause.

Within six months of her first post about Mili and the spectacles, Sonia was logging at least 1,500 likes per post. She no longer even bothered to check her phone until the four-digit number had been crossed. People started sending her stuff: clothes for Mili, toys for her child, a real pair of funky sunglasses, an apron and a chef's hat. Small businesses reached out to her, asking if she could please have Mili pose with their organic jams, or skin-friendly scouring powder.

'Well I want to do what's right for her, and it's only fair that you pay her for these pictures,' she'd write back. Her charges rose from 1,500 rupees a post to 6,000 rupees. A kitchenware company paid her 30,000 rupees a month to have their products in the background of these pictures. Of course, Mili had no idea about any of this. She noticed a sharp rise in the number of photos she was now made to pose for, but having worked in dozens of homes for dozens of years, Mili knew that employers were eccentric, their tempers and husbands were to be feared, and their idiosyncrasies ignored.

One day she arrived at work with the bruises of her own husband's routine beating shining purple on her face. Sonu madam brought out some lipstick and other make-up and called her over to the mirror. There, using her fingers and a brush, Madam proceeded to make the area near her eye blacker and the welt on her chin redder, before taking a few pictures of her face up close. 'Go, wash it off,' she said afterwards, and even Mili recognized that a subtle line between idiosyncrasy and insanity had been crossed.

Sonia then posted: 'This is how Mili came to work today. Her husband is an alcoholic and has beaten her up. I am distraught. Girls please tell me what to do.' The comments came flooding in. Some asked her to take Mili to the police, others to visit her home and talk to her husband. Some helpfully provided phone numbers of de-addiction clinics. Sonia thanked them all individually. 'Leaving now for police station and then de-addiction clinic,' she wrote at the bottom, before yelling at Mili to stop wasting time looking at the mirror and lay the table for lunch instead.

With the success of her #MyMili hashtag, Sonia was beginning to be recognized in markets and malls. It was thrilling at first, but then she began to worry. What would happen if they came up to her when she was with her husband, who did not even know that she was Sonia Sarm? When she went to Rishi's school for the parent–teacher meeting, a few mothers looked at her strangely, as though they had seen her somewhere but couldn't quite place where.

What if people found and approached Mili? The maid worked at two other apartments in the building—one was occupied by an elderly couple and the other by a single man. Neither of them was likely to be on the Facebook group, but for a while, Sonia stopped posting pictures of Mili or herself, just to be on the safe side. But no one seemed to read posts without the bait of an accompanying image. It was virtually impossible to get traction without pictures. And the brands that approached her wouldn't pay anything for posts that didn't feature photographs.

In the middle of all this, as if things weren't tiresome enough for Sonia, Mili started demanding a raise. She was getting paid 2,500 rupees a month, for 'a few minutes of work' as Sonia thought of it. And now she wanted 3,500 rupees. Sonia opened up her calculator and showed Mili the numbers. 'See that's a 40 per cent raise. Even my husband who works in an office will never get a 40 per cent raise. Stop talking nonsense, Mili. I look after you so well, and you are demanding so much money from me? Go and work in a house where they talk to you like a servant, then you will know my value.'

'But Didi, my husband met with an accident. He can't even stand up for more than a few minutes now. He won't be able to go back to riding his rickshaw for months. How will we eat, Didi?' Mili pleaded. And back and forth, they went.

Finally, Sonia agreed to a 100-rupee raise. Mili sulked for a while, banging the vessels and 'forgetting' to take out the trash. The next time she walked in with a black eye and a split lip, Sonia simply ignored her. 'My man is unable to go to work and every day he fights with me for money to buy liquor,' Mili said, hoping, if nothing else, for at least a sympathetic 'tut-tut'. But, Sonia walked into her bedroom and shut the door. When it happened a second time in the same week, Sonia said, 'You should also think about your attitude, Mili. You have the habit of annoying people, maybe you don't realize it.'

'Wondering what to buy Mili for her birthday next week,' she posted that day, accompanied by a blurry picture of the back of Mili's head. It didn't set the group on fire, though there was a discussion on bonuses for the help and how some people knew other people who fired their maids a week before Diwali just to get out of having to pay them any. A couple of local sari shops and a pressure-cooker brand reached out to her to for possible collaborations. So it wasn't too bad.

By the time the New Year came around, Sonia's relationship with Mili had reverted to a grudging peace. The maid's bachelor employer had moved out, so Mili could be tasked with more work around the house—clean the top of the fridge, refold the clothes in the cupboard, wipe the windows from outside—even though Mili tried to fake a fear of heights. Yes, the parapet was narrow and it was a sheer drop from the seventh floor, but all the other maids were doing it, so why should Mili be such a drama queen? (Indeed, Sonia had once taken a photo of her neighbour's maid on the parapet and posted an indignant message about how some people didn't care about the help's safety. The early comments complimented her sense of social justice. But then a group of women talked about coming together and filing a police complaint against the employer. That would have been an unmitigated disaster; she would have had to tell them where she lived and troop along to the station with them. Rishi had tuitions and needed his tiffin. Where did she have the time? Luckily, someone else diverted their attention to something else.)

By Holi, things had settled into a rhythm. A new ice-lolly brand struck a deal with Sonia for posts all through the hot months. There were promising discussions with a distributor of baking accessories, easy-to-dust furniture and even some bed-linen people. With the fight over the raise forgotten and Sonia implementing the important lesson not to let the servants think you are their friend, things were on an even keel.

Lulled into a sense of complacency, she did not even notice the first two days in the week when Mili came in late for work. On the third day, she had a hot photo idea ready and was raring for Mili to arrive. Only then she noticed that it was past ten-thirty, with no Mili in sight.

She finally did roll in at eleven, as though nothing was wrong. 'Why are you late?' Sonia asked her at the door. Mili walked past her and went straight to the kitchen. 'You are supposed to be here before ten-thirty. Just because I didn't say anything the last two days, don't take advantage of me, Mili.'

'Didi, I'll have to come at eleven every day now,' Mili replied tersely. 'There is a new family that's moved into the bachelor's house. They want me from nine to eleven.'

'Sorry Mili, you have to adjust your new work around your existing schedule. I am your old employer. You can't expect me to dance around your new job. You can start there earlier and finish by ten-thirty, or go there in the afternoon,' Sonia snapped.

'Sorry, Didi,' Mili said, 'but I can't start work there until Sir leaves for office, and afternoon is too late. You only have to adjust for half an hour. I finish all my work here before lunchtime anyway. And besides,' Mili paused for effect, 'she is paying me 3,500 rupees. Plus full Diwali bonus, even though I would have worked only half a year by then.'

Sonia's heart sank. Over the following weeks, Mili started to press harder on this theme. The new didi had given her new sandals and four as-good-as-new sarees. The new didi had taken her out to watch a film the previous evening. The new didi paid her children's school fees. Sonia mostly listened wordlessly, but she also tried to shake things up. She and Mili posed for some crazy pictures. She went through her cupboard and gave the maid some old T-shirts she hadn't worn in years. When she went to the market, she bought Mili a 50-rupee pair of earrings with bright orange beads. 'Your honeymoon with the new didi will end, Mili, and then you'll only have me,' she warned, as she handed over the danglers. Mili nodded her head in agreement, but the spectre of the new didi hung in the air between them.

One Tuesday, Mili didn't turn up for work. She did not even call. Sonia tried her number a few times but the calls went unanswered. Sonia had a strict system for sanctioned days off and it had worked well so far. Two Sundays off a month, fifteen days of unpaid holidays to go to the village and a deduction of two days' pay for every day of unannounced absence. Mili had rarely taken a day off. If she called in the morning with a story about a sick child or a pain in the stomach, Sonia would coolly agree to the holiday, but remind her about the pay cut. Mili often came to work right away, exaggeratedly dragging a foot or breathing heavily.

When there was no sign of her by noon, Sonia called the new didi's home on the intercom. 'Hello, I am enquiring about Mili. Did she come in today?' she asked. 'Oh hello, Mili has told me so much about you. I've been meaning to come over and introduce myself. It's unfortunate though that we have to speak under these circumstances. You see, Mili came in the morning looking terrible. Her cheek was swollen and her nose was bleeding. It seems her husband drank too much and beat her up all night, poor thing. So I took her to the doctor in the morning, and then sent her home. The doctor said she needs her rest.'

Sonia was seething. But she managed to mutter some polite words and hung up. Who did this woman think she was? Florence Nightingale? She set about doing the dishes, dipping her hands into plates crusted with last night's food, trying not to retch. Disgusting.

When Mili came to work the next day, she was bursting with the excitement of having ridden in the new didi's car to the doctor's, showing scant remorse about the unscheduled day off. Sonia had two deadlines for the week—both the pressure cooker and ice-lolly photos were due. So without a word she handed Mili the lolly and asked her to taste it. Click click. She quickly took a shot of their heads together, a lolly in each of their hands. Mili's eyes were closed in anticipation of the cold.

Sonia uploaded the picture with the caption that the company had prepared for her. 'Spread the joy with people who matter.' She should have made Mili look a bit better though. Maybe applied some make-up, so the commentators would be able to see how well looked after she was.

Thankfully the lolly hid the crust that had formed under the maid's bloodied nose.

Sonia watched the likes roll in. The pleasure of that was still so real. And then, the comments began. 'You two are the best', 'People should learn from you', 'Stay blessed.' She sat glued to the speech bubbles waiting for the comments to appear. Ting ting ting. Sonia smiled as each new comment popped up.

And then she saw, 'OMG that's Mili, who works in my home.' The profile picture was of a dumpy, dark-skinned woman posing with her husband in a foreign country. A shiver went down Sonia's spine. She knew exactly how things were going to unfold going forward. Who had allowed this new didi into the group? How could she get her out? Could she block her profile? All day, Sonia worried about what to do. The new didi was likely to show Mili the posts. The new didi could uncover all kinds of truths. The new didi would certainly be a virtue warrior. There was nothing Sonia could do to stop the new didi from damaging her celebrity and her reputation.

It was with a heavy heart that Sonia picked up the phone and dialled the number for the security guard's cabin. 'I don't want to make a big deal out of this, but the maid, Mili, has stolen my diamond earrings, a watch and some money. Please don't allow her into the building from tomorrow.' She hung up. If Mili made a scene, she'd be forced to take her to the police station. She hoped it wouldn't come to that. She heard herself exhale, long and loud. Then she sat down to compose her goodbye post to Mili.

Before the Flight

ANNIE ZAIDI

Wind may screech into your armpit
There's nowhere much better
It's not as if the rivers care
And the fish have nowhere
To go

Say then, you have wings
And pity the fish trapped
In their silken cage of water but
Go, you must

Treetops may send caution
Flight is not all
Nest, a bend of limb
Could be home

Say then, you are at home
In flight and in tree
Say, roots are not the thing
that bind but set free

To frost, say, you are welcome
But not in my blood
To salt, say, you are beloved
But not my keeper

When sisters say, we stay
The land holds us in peace
It yields plenty
See?

Say, bless you
Sisters, watch me dance
Watch the sky yield
Butter to my sword heart.

Requiem for the Siberian Crane

SWAMINATHAN S. ANKLESARIA AIYAR

In my younger days, I used to go almost every winter to the Keoladeo bird sanctuary near Bharatpur, four hours from New Delhi. It was a marvellous place, with enormous marshes and lakes holding a multitude of water birds, from kingfishers, lapwings and mallards, to herons, storks and cormorants. Bee-eaters, drongos and blue jays flitted from treetops to electric wires. But the sanctuary's pride of place belonged to the Siberian crane.

A rare visitor from the Siberian tundra, it travelled thousands of miles across the Himalayas to winter in Indian lakes. Alas, the migratory population began to dwindle over the years, because of water scarcity and loss of habitat. Eventually the cranes stopped coming altogether. The Indian environment, once so welcoming to weary aerial nomads, had become so hostile that they abandoned their centuries-old migratory habits.

That disaster echoed in my mind when I heard of the horrific gangrape and murder of Asifa Bano, an eight-year-old girl from a nomadic tribe in Kashmir, the Muslim Bakarwals. The Bakarwals grazed goats and sheep in high alpine meadows in the Himalayas in summer, and then came down in the winter to the warmer climes of Jammu. Like the Siberian cranes, they had made this migratory journey for hundreds of years. Like the Siberian cranes, this age-old migration was suddenly threatened by a hostile environment.

In place of the old Hindu–Muslim amity, new Hindu fundamentalist forces stoked hate of Muslims. So entrenched did this become that a group of Hindus saw themselves as community heroes when they gangraped and killed Asifa, a deliberately horrific act aimed at terrifying the Bakarwals so much that they would stop coming to that village in winter. The killers succeeded: the Bakarwals no longer come.

What has happened to my country? How can the most despicable acts be equated with community pride? Communal hate is not new of course; it has always simmered below the surface. And yet the Hinduism I grew up with was, despite many aberrations, a fundamentally tolerant and multi-faceted faith, willing to not just accommodate but celebrate diversity.

When India went to war with Pakistan in 1971, General Sam Manekshaw, a Parsi, led the army. The assistant air chief was Idris Latif, a Muslim. The Eastern Front commander who captured Dhaka was Jagjit Singh Aurora, a Sikh, His chief of staff was Lieutenant-General Jack Jacob, a Jew. What they wrought was not a Hindu victory over Muslims, but a secular Indian victory in which people of all faiths could rejoice.

Those days look distant now. Hindu communalism has moved from the wings to centre stage. Lip service is still paid to the ideal that all Indians are one regardless of religion, but there can be no mistake about the desire to create a Hindu state in which minorities are second-class citizens. Muslims and Christians are fearful and cowed, losing faith in the ability or willingness of the state to protect their life and liberty. Liberals and the independent media are under pressure, intimidated by tax raids, bogus criminal cases, withdrawal of advertising revenue and other economic pressures. The mere possibility of harsh consequences has led to self-censorship, with journalists preferring to avoid direct criticism of Narendra Modi or Amit Shah.

This has destroyed the vision of India conjured by Rabindranath Tagore:

> Where the mind is without fear and the head is held high
> Where knowledge is free
> Where the world has not been broken up into fragments
> By narrow domestic walls
> Where words come out from the depth of truth
> Where tireless striving stretches its arms towards perfection
> Where the clear stream of reason has not lost its way
> Into the dreary desert sand of dead habit
> Where the mind is led forward by thee
> Into ever-widening thought and action
> Into that heaven of freedom,
> My Father, let my country awake.

The India we see today is very different. It is a place where the mind is full of fear and the head is held discreetly low; where knowledge is too dangerous to be shared freely; where the country has deliberately been broken into fragments by narrow domestic walls of religion; where words come out of the depths of opportunism; where tireless striving stretches its arms towards communalism; where the clear stream of reason has been told to go take a 'sickular' hike; into that cesspit of unfreedom, my father, has my country fallen. It truly needs an awakening.

Paper Cranes

GURMEHAR KAUR

Ruhi sat at the last desk of her classroom, doodling in her notebook. Drawing floral patterns in the corners, losing herself in the meditative quality of drawing was a better activity for her mental health than focusing on the equations being taught in the maths class. She hated maths with a vengeance. Since physics and chemistry were also taught by the same teacher, by default, she hated those too. It was a Tuesday. The only class today that did not make her want her to jump out of the window and run far away from the uncomfortable wooden desks, with their ugly compass engraving carved by her predecessors, across the cricket field and through the gardens, to a little corner behind the chapel where she spent most of her lunch breaks was moral science.

This was an important subject in her Catholic school. A way to teach kids the way of life as God would have it. But to her it was simply about reading stories and chatting with the teacher. She wondered if the class toppers who often bullied and mocked her for her mediocre academic achievements actually understood what was being taught in those lectures. The textbook they studied was full of stories that were far from reality. In those stories the nuns and teachers were kind people who helped young kids to grow and learn about life. Children were upheld as God's own special creations, a symbol of innocence.

She might have only been alive for fourteen years, but she knew that all of this was a lie. She did not know much of the world beyond the playground and her school, but what she did know was that it was nothing like the moral science teacher made it out to be. No one was going to return a 10-rupee note found on the playing field during recess. And no one was going to be completely honest and tell the teacher the reason that they had not finished their homework was because they had chosen to watch TV instead. In reality, they would take that 10-rupee note and buy themselves a Pepsi at the school canteen; they would lie through their teeth about their incomplete homework, claiming a family member's fictitious illness.

'Ruhi, what are you doing? Show me your notebook!'

She looked up from her desk at her teacher's large, saggy face, forehead scrunched into a frown and nose flaring. 'Sorry, ma'am. It's nothing,' she muttered quickly, trying to put away the notebook, but her teacher was too fast. Snatching at the notebook, she opened it to the page where Ruhi had drawn a sketch of the garden she'd have liked to be sitting in, instead of in the maths class. There were rose mallows scattered across the notebook, and zinnias sprouting from the corners into the centre of the page.

'This is what you have been doing?' The teacher slammed her heavy, sweaty hand on the desk, leaving a chalky imprint behind. 'Tell me!' She shouted into Ruhi's young face, as it grew smaller and redder with embarrassment.

'No, ma'am,' Ruhi managed to mumble.

'Go to the board right now and solve the problem,' she ordered. Ruhi knew that this was the teacher's way of humiliating her, but she did not understand why anyone would want to do this to their student. Did the teacher not realize that this kind of bullying only gave a free pass to everyone else to treat her the same way? Or was that in fact why she did it?

Ruhi shuffled up to the blackboard, picking up a piece of chalk from the teacher's table on the way. She did not bother to read the question. Instead she played the part she was supposed to play. After staring blankly at the board for a few seconds, she turned around and apologized. 'Sorry, ma'am, I don't know the answer.'

'Class, look at what this girl has been doing instead of maths,' the teacher said, holding up the notebook, serving up Ruhi's personal thoughts, her tiny world of flowers, to the entire group of 56 kids for their amusement. Predictably, the class burst into laughter. 'Shameful! Your parents send you to study and this is what you do? Now go back to your desk and study, or else I will call your parents. Stop with this nonsense drawing immediately.'

She hated this place, Ruhi thought as she slowly made her way back to her desk. A few minutes later the bell rang and it was time for her moral-science class. Thank God for Tuesdays.

*

Ruhi was rummaging through her bag when she looked up and found a tiny paper bird sitting on her desk, a small message asking her to open it scrawled on its wing. She looked at the crane suspiciously and then scanned the classroom to locate this latest prankster. She had had enough of this school, of this teacher, of her father and mother, both of whom refused to stand up for her. Part of her wanted to throw the paper crane in the dustbin, but another part wanted to unfold it and see what was inside.

Curiosity got the better of her. After all, how much worse could the day get? She picked the bird up and gently began opening it up in her lap, hands hidden under the desk.

'Verma is mean to everyone. I saw you drew the chapel garden, didn't know anyone else knew it existed. It's my favourite place too. I'll show you something there.' The note was signed off: 'Sahir'.

Sahir was the golden boy of the class, who never uttered a word out of turn and was every teacher's favourite. Even his hair was always properly combed to stay in place, unlike her unruly mop. In fact, he was everything her parents hoped, in vain, that she would be. Sahir had been in the same class as her since Class I and there was a time they had been friendly. But as they'd grown up she had begun to hate school and taken to keeping to herself. Sahir wasn't much of a talker either, but unlike her he wasn't one to cause trouble in class.

Ruhi looked up from the message and glanced across the rows of desks between her seat and his. She met his eye. He smiled and quickly looked away just as the teacher entered the classroom. Today, the teacher announced, they would read a story about empathy.

*

'It was really pretty, the drawing,' he said when they met in the hall after school let out.

'Thank you,' she replied, her bag hanging from her shoulder, eyes squinting up at him. Ruhi knew that he wouldn't mock her like the other kids. He wasn't friendly with the boys who made fun of the length of her hair or the length of her skirt, who thought that just because the teachers made fun of her constantly, they could too.

'Why are you being nice to me?' she asked abruptly.

'Oh!' He paused for a moment. 'I just genuinely did not know anyone else who knew that the garden existed. I thought maybe you would like to see this secret place near there that I found one day when I went to drop off some notebooks to the staff room on that side.'

'OK,' she said after a pause.

'OK,' he agreed, now a little unsure about whether he had crossed a line.

He hated the way Verma treated Ruhi in class. It was unfair. The way her face fell when the kids laughed at her made him feel ashamed. Who knew what was going on with her? She almost never spoke to anyone and was always buried in a vampire novel. He just wanted to be friendly.

'So, lead the way,' Ruhi said as they started walking.

Following at her heels he mumbled, 'Sorry about Verma. She can be so mean.'

'Yeah, I hate her the most . . .'

'I can see why . . .'

'I hate this whole class. I hate this whole world. I just want to leave this school . . .' Ruhi began to rant but stopped herself mid-sentence. 'Wait, why would you say that? Aren't you her favourite?'

'Yes, but it still isn't fair that she treats anyone like that, no?'

Ruhi knew she had found a friend. That it was the first day of a friendship that would last for a very long time.

Every day after that one, Ruhi and Sahir would meet up after class and go to the gardens. She would write in her journal or read her vampire books and he would finish his homework for the day. After a few days, she readily opened up and told him about her father who was always absent, away on foreign work trips. About her mother, a wedding planner who was always waiting for her husband's return. About their constant bickering and her fear that she might have to pick between the two someday soon. If push came to shove, Ruhi would pick her mother for sure.

She said this out loud for the first time to him when they were eating Maggi noodles from his tiffin box that were left over from lunch. 'I would pick her too,' he said not knowing what this meant, but knowing that he agreed with her.

Slowly, she found out more about him. His father owned a huge general store near Jama Masjid, one of the biggest mosques in the Old Delhi area. The store had been passed down the generations in the family.

'So, you will also become a shopkeeper?' she asked him jokingly.

'Of course not!' he laughed. 'I will become a pilot.'

'And who will take care of your store when you're off flying planes?'

'My dad, at least until he's old. After that I'll be a rich pilot and hire managers who'll send me accounts every month. I'll just oversee the work.'

'From *over seas*?' she teased.

'So lame, Ruhi! Why are you so lame?' He laughed again. 'Yes I will *oversee* it all from overseas.'

*

Sahir took the metro home that day rather than the school bus. The station was a short walk away from the school, but it was only very recently that his parents had felt he was old enough to travel on his own. Now that he was fourteen, his face had sprouted a few hairs on the chin and his voice had finally begun to break. The world was finally his for the taking.

Ruhi's mother picked her up every day after school. Since the day of the Verma showdown, Ruhi had asked her mother to collect her an hour later than usual. 'Music society,' she'd mumbled casually. As for Sahir, no one asked him any questions. He was a boy. And so they both settled into a comfortable schedule.

It wasn't often that they hung out on the weekends because Sahir had to help out at the store and Ruhi often accompanied her mother to the weddings that she organized. Ruhi liked tagging along to the receptions for the free food and the few sips of alcohol she could sneak when no one was looking. She told Sahir about her little rebellions one day and invited him to come along to the next party.

'I can go with you to a wedding, if you like, but I can't drink. I'm Muslim and it's not cool in our religion,' he'd said matter-of-factly.

'What? You take all that seriously?' she asked.

'I don't know. I'm not really interested in religion too much,' he'd replied.

'Fair enough,' she'd said with a wink. 'But when in doubt, you can always ask me. I'm a pro!'

Sahir had never felt particularly 'Muslim'. He had felt a lot of things when he was around Ruhi: happy and full of life; even lost and angry. But he'd never felt Muslim. Then one day he took the metro home and everything changed.

His family lived on the floor above their store. Everyday he would come home to his father sitting at his desk on the shop floor, reading a newspaper or chitchatting with a customer. But on this day, for the first time in years, he found the shutters to the ground-floor shop pulled down. There was no way to go inside the house, since the stairs that led up to their apartment passed through the shop. He continued to bang on the shutters. The street was abnormally silent. Wondering what had happened, he kept banging, until his fists hurt. His gut told him that whatever this was, it was not good news. He called out his father's name a few more times but to no avail.

He went over all the things that could have happened and he tried not to think of the worst. On the verge of tears, he saw his neighbour's scooter drive up the street. 'Bhaiyya, do you know where Mummy–Papa are?' he asked frantically. Mohit was a tutor who coached aspiring Class XII commerce students. He'd known Sahir since he was a baby and had been somewhat of a mentor to the boy as he'd grown up.

But today Mohit did not meet Sahir's questioning eyes. 'Your mother was hit,' he mumbled.

The blood drained from Sahir's face. Images of his mother lying blood-ied on the side of the road flashed in his mind. Why would anyone 'hit' her? What did that even mean? She was just a simple housewife. He thought of his mother's warm eyes, of her laughter reverberating through the walls of the house.

'Is she OK?' he finally managed to ask, steeling himself for the worst.

'She's fine. But she was attacked by a mob of young boys on her way back from the bazaar,' Mohit replied, trying to find words to explain what had happened.

'But why would anyone want to attack her? What did she have? What did she do?' Sahir asked, momentarily relieved, yet confused and angry all at the same time.

Mohit continued to look down. 'They wanted to pull your mother's burqa off because they thought it would be fun,' he finally said. 'She tried to stop them and tripped. Her head hit the corner of a cart that was parked there.'

He paused and finally looked up at Sahir. 'Instead of helping her, the boys told her to go back to "her" country, Pakistan.' His voice quivered. 'Then they laughed and ran away.'

In the days that followed, Sahir was angry all the time. He threw things. He told everyone who listened that he would find those boys and beat them up. He thought up elaborate revenge fantasies.

When the anger ran out, he cried.

He cried for the loss of his innocence, because he'd finally realized that he was different. He thought of his friends, his school, and his teachers. He thought of Ruhi and he cried. We are not the same, he told himself. We never were. He did not go to school that whole week and avoided Ruhi's calls.

Ruhi eventually found out what had happened when she overheard a group of teachers talking about it in the corridors. She knew she had to speak to Sahir as soon as possible. To tell him that she was sorry, even though she did not know what she had to be sorry about. Yet, she was desperately sorry. She couldn't imagine something so terrible happening to someone she knew. These were things she'd only read about in newspapers before.

She thought about all the ways in which Sahir and her were different. He didn't drink alcohol. She loved bacon. Then, almost immediately, she thought about what they shared. They both liked iced tea and chicken pizza. They enjoyed the chapel garden. They hated Verma. They both loved starry night skies.

That day Ruhi left a paper crane on Sahir's desk with a message that asked him to open it.

Parable of Cyclone, 2019

MANU DASH

1

Here: a white-knuckled parable of our times.
A devastating cyclone
Soon after the last leg of national and state polling were over,
Soon after the missiles of scathing abuses slamming both sides came
to an end,
Soon after the claims of the ruling and opposition party to have
gained an absolute majority were done with,
Soon after the Sturm und Drang of choosing between the yell and
teardrop of the crocodile were over,
The cyclone visited our bucolic region.
It drops in more often than politicians do at their constituencies.

2

The announcement of its arrival was repeated for days
Accompanied by a litany of dos and don'ts
Long queues formed for a share of potatoes
And for essential commodities about to vanish from the market—
Candlesticks, matchboxes, beaten rice, battery torches, hand fans,

water bottles, biscuits, baby food, sanitary napkins, kerosene.
Like perfume seeping from an uncorked bottle into the air,
Creating panic and price hikes.

3
The cyclone arrived and disappeared as scheduled,
The PM surveyed the distressed areas as scheduled,
The CM issued appeals every day urging calm, as scheduled,
People suffered, as scheduled.

The summer was at its hottest.
In the evening, I climbed up to the terrace for some respite,
And stared at the blazing stars in the sky.
They gazed back at me,
And slowly turned into paper cranes bearing the message
That this cyclone was not merely a cyclone,
But a biopsy of our society.

(Un)Folding Secrets

THE CONTENTS OF MY MOTHER'S CHINESE CHEST

JONATHAN GIL HARRIS

There are many ways of folding a piece of paper. And many motivations for folding it. One can fold it into something beautiful—an origami crane. But one can also fold it to avert one's gaze from what is contained in it. Folding can be creative; it can be a mode of avoidance. It can be both simultaneously.

When I was growing up in New Zealand, a particularly striking piece of furniture dominated my family's otherwise sparse living room: a large Chinese chest, built of sturdy teak and bearing on its sides and lid the most remarkable bas-relief wood carvings of monkish men in robes. At the edges of each of the sides and lid were deep crenelated grooves containing intricate patterns. As a small boy I spent a lot of time gazing at the monks, tracing the patterned lines, absent-mindedly smelling the chest's faint but distinctive woody odour. All these sparked in me an inchoate longing for Asia. That longing arguably led to one of my most important life choices many years later. At the time, though, my only conscious wish was to know what was hidden in the chest. But I never opened it. Or, more accurately, I *almost* never opened it.

My mother had forbidden us to do so. The chest was the one heirloom that connected her to her pre-war childhood in Warsaw. I knew that it was crammed full of photos and letters, written in Polish and German, from family members I'd never met, some of them exterminated in the Nazi death camps. The letters were all folded within envelopes; the photos were stuffed in other envelopes, which had been tucked into the envelopes containing the letters. Folded memorabilia, hidden in receptacles within receptacles. Folded memorabilia, in other words, stranded in a limbo between remembrance and oblivion. I knew all this because I had snuck a few peeks inside the chest when my mother was not looking. The contents of the chest were a jumbled mess: the envelopes holding the letters and photos were buried willy-nilly in shredded paper and naphthalene like items in a horror-show lucky dip. I was dissuaded from excavating too much as the stench of naphtha would stink out the entire living room if the lid was left ajar even for a moment. I have a vague memory of opening the lid and, within seconds, my mother—summoned by the smell like a horrified genie from a lamp—ran in with a cry to slam it shut again.

That closed chest became, for my sisters and me, a mute emblem of my mother's childhood trauma. Her trauma was always undeniably, forcefully present in our lives. Yet its contents were beyond scrutiny. My mother's past was folded to us.

As time unfolded, though, the Chinese chest too began to unfold some of its secrets.

*

Even before Alzheimer's destroyed her memory, my mother was a champion history-folder. Stella Freud had survived the Holocaust that killed almost every member of her family. Yet she always denied that she was a Holocaust survivor. She did so not just because she hadn't ended up in the death camps of Poland and Germany where most of her cousins, grandparents, aunts and uncles had been deported, but also because—or so she maintained—her wartime experiences had been among the very happiest of her life.

Stella had been born into a bourgeois Jewish family in Warsaw in 1934. The extended Freud family traced, through its business activities, a profoundly cosmopolitan network across many borders: Stella's sister Mariska had been born in Bucharest, her mother had been born in Vienna, and she had uncles and aunts scattered across the Ukraine, Romania, Turkey and Palestine. The Freuds' bourgeois fashion sense combined with their business connections made for a steady flow of exotic Asian commodities into their homes. Stella's favourite uncle, Joe, lived in Palestine, fetishized anything Persian, painted Bengali women, and purchased that Chinese chest. Many years later, I found in the chest a photo of my grandmother wearing a Japanese kimono; in another photo, my mother's Uncle Janek reclines on a couch in the languorous pose of an Ottoman pasha, surrounded by Persian carpets.

Despite this well-heeled milieu, full of eye-catching oriental baubles, Stella always narrated her pre-war childhood as a time of privation. She dearly loved her father Nathan Freud, a warm, smiling man who sang to her and called her Stellusia. But he was more often than not away on business trips to Istanbul or Sofia or Vienna. Her mother Lola was a committed socialite who preferred shopping expeditions and the company of high-class women friends in the city's coffee shops to time with her daughters, which she largely outsourced to nannies. My mother's older sister, perhaps feeling keenly the absence of both parents, often beat Stella—as did a succession of strict governesses. When the parents were at home, it was usually in the company of friends and relatives in the receiving room, to which the two girls were strictly barred entry.

This barrier was linguistic as much as physical. In the Freud house on Warsaw's Granicza Street, a well-off neighbourhood just two blocks away from Saxon Gardens, the city's central park, different languages were spoken in different rooms. In the family room, my mother spoke Polish with her parents and nanny. But she spoke Romanian in her shared bedroom with her Bucharest-born sister; Yiddish in the kitchen and vestibule with her cook; and French—the language of etiquette—in the dining room. She understood German, but had no occasion to speak it herself. For it was the language her parents spoke when they were in the receiving room, talking to each other and to their guests about adult matters from which Stella and Mariska were excluded. German was the language of no-entry.

One day in 1937, there was a great deal of excited chatter among the adults in the Freuds' house. My mother—ear pressed to the door of the receiving room—was puzzled by it all. 'Twój wujek przyjdie jutro,' she was informed by her father when he swept out out and saw her, Your uncle is coming tomorrow. My mother had a lot of uncles who passed through town, so the news didn't strike her as being anything out of the ordinary. But through the closed door to the receiving room, she overheard the other adults continue to chatter animatedly about this uncle in German, not Polish. And one German word they used stuck in her memory: *Traumdeutung*, dream theory. In my mother's mind, this mysterious Freud uncle became *Traumonkel*, dream uncle. To a little girl from a family where parents led their own strange German-speaking lives, the idea of a dream uncle was a rather appealing one. She was in any case longing for a dream mother and a dream father who would be available to her all the time.

The next day, Traumonkel came to the house—and was quickly spirited away into the adult domain of the receiving room. Through the door my mother could hear the murmurs of her father and uncle. But they felt impossibly far away, not least because the conversation was taking so long. Her disappointment converted into irritation, her irritation into anger, her anger into impatience. Finally little Stella threw all caution to the wind. She opened the door to the forbidden room and, against the warnings of her nanny and sister, marched in. 'Chcę porozmawiać z tatusiem!'—I want to talk to Daddy!—she announced as she caught her first glimpse of Traumonkel, an old cigar-scented man with a white beard and pebble glasses. She clambered into his lap so she could glare more effectively at her daddy. Her father waved her away. But Traumonkel said, 'lass das Kind bleiben, Nathan,' let the child stay, Nathan. She remained sitting in Traumonkel's lap for the rest of his visit—sitting, folded, on an Uncle Freud canonized by history yet folded out of her view, so she could gaze at the father she loved and missed.

We fold to dwell in fantasy. And we dwell in fantasy in the hope of a better world. My mother folded away her uncle, in the hope of connecting more fully with her father. I too am folding here: folding, if not a crane, then a story out of bits of stray paper from the Chinese chest, including a small photo of an old man with a white beard and pebble glasses, in the hope of connecting with a larger family I never knew, and in the hope of reconstituting something of what was shattered by the war.

*

Shortly after the German invasion of western Poland in September 1939, Nathan Freud—who some months earlier had been conscripted to serve in the Polish army—deserted. He moved his wife and two daughters to Lvov, in Soviet-occupied Poland, where they holed up with his mother, two brothers, their wives, daughters and daughters' children. For Nathan and Lola, the move couldn't have been anything other than a shocking disruption. Used to the luxury of their palatial apartment in Warsaw, sharing a smaller house with a large extended family surely represented for them a considerable loss of prestige as well as personal space. For five-year-old Stella, however, it was a liberation into a world of human connections she had fiercely coveted all her life. In particular, she revelled in the company of her cousin Lusia's little three-year-old son Ludwig, known as Viki. She mothered and smothered Viki, treating him as her personal human doll, caressing and clutching him for hours at a time.

Sometime in the spring of 1940, six months into their Lvov exile, Nathan Freud made a fateful decision. He was no doubt longing for the comforts of his house in Granizca Street; he was also heartened by 'news'— read: wishful thinking fashioned out of the folds of pure fantasy—that the German occupation wasn't as bad as everyone had feared it would be. The fantasy was not just his. Others, Jews as much as Gentiles, wanted to avert their gaze from the horrors unfolding and the certainty of even worse horrors to come. Nathan was only happy to follow their lead. He announced that he would be moving his daughters and wife back to Warsaw.

As daft as Nathan's decision was, it probably saved Stella's life. A few days after leaving Lvov, Nathan, Lola, Mariska and Stella were detained by the Soviet authorities at the border with German-occupied western Poland. The German invasion of Warsaw had been enabled by the

Molotov–Ribbentrop Pact of August 1939, in which Stalin received a promise from Hitler of non-aggression between their two countries in exchange for Soviet control of territories in eastern Poland and German control of the west. In the Soviet-occupied part of Poland, desertion from the national army was a crime; Nathan, Lola, and the girls were promptly deported as anti-nationals to a Russian camp near Archangelsk, in the Arctic Circle, for Poles. They had unwittingly dodged a bullet. In June of 1941, the German army broke the Molotov–Ribbentrop Pact and invaded eastern Poland, including Lvov. All the members of the Freud household in Lvov were deported to Auschwitz. Save one: little Viki died when the Germans came to their house.

Many years later, my mother began to receive letters from her cousin Lusia, Viki's mother. Lusia alone among the Lvov Freuds had managed to survive her time in Auschwitz; she had been a rare beauty, and rumour had it that she was spared death because she had become the mistress of one of the camp commandants. Astonishingly, Lusia settled after the war in Bielsko-Biała, a city just five miles from Auschwitz. There she married a Christian Pole and had another child. She folded her past from view, even as she kept it close to hand—a horrific version of my mother's Chinese chest. In 2006 I visited Lusia's daughter in Bielsko-Biała, lured in part by her promise that we had 'so much of the past to catch up on'; but it turned out she knew nothing of her mother's war experiences. For her, the 'past' didn't include anything before 1950; it meant skiing trips she had taken in southern Poland in the 1980s and 1990s.

Living in the shadow of Auschwitz, Lusia remained incommunicado for years, muzzled not just by the Iron Curtain but also by the folds of her trauma. But in the 1960s she felt a need to reach out to my mother, the one other survivor of her shattered family. She wrote Stella a letter that my mother, upon receiving it, immediately stuffed in the Chinese chest, along with a photo that Lusia had enclosed. In it, Lusia sits with her Polish husband; you can still make out something of the extraordinary beauty that had impressed my mother thirty years earlier in Lvov. But Lusia wears a haunted look. Perhaps something of that haunting prompted her to write a follow-up letter to my mother, in which she unfolded what had happened the day Germans arrived at the Freud house in Lvov in June 1941. She told my mother that Viki had been taken from her and ripped apart in front of her eyes by two Nazi soldiers.

Stella folded Lusia's last letter. And then burned it. She never revealed its contents to her children; she didn't reveal them many years later to her psychotherapist, with whom she had made a clinically improbable pact never to speak about her childhood. A pact, as its Latin root (*pax*, or peace) suggests, is an agreement driven by a longing for peace. But the Molotov–Ribbentrop Pact is a reminder that a pact can also be an act of folding designed to conceal secrets from view—the secret of aggressive ambitions, the secret of violence. Burning the letter was part of a pact my mother had made with her family history to keep its most traumatic parts secret. I found out what Lusia had written in her letter only many years later, when my father haltingly shared with me something he had overheard decades earlier from my mother. She hadn't deliberately opened up to him about what had happened to Viki. He had gleaned it by accident: at the height of her distress, in the middle of a sleepless night, she had muttered aloud to herself about Viki's murder.

Stella had been spared full knowledge of Viki's fate for three decades. But she had also been spared full knowledge of her own. She was only five at the time of her Russian deportation, which she experienced—or so she told us—as a joyful adventure. Lola Freud plummeted into depression, horrified by the change in their material circumstances. No more Japanese kimonos for her, though she had managed to smuggle out of Granicza Street some of the expensive family silverware, with which she continued to eat the lean fare available in the camp. But Stella, at least according to the narrative she chose to share with us, tasted liberation in the Arctic. She was able to go mushrooming and berrying in the forest, and have her mother and father to herself. She folded away her parents' trauma in order to connect with them.

*

My sisters and I always regarded our mother's narrative about her supposedly halcyon days in the Archangelsk camp with great scepticism. It was Exhibit A in her long-standing case that she was not to be regarded as a Holocaust survivor—a case she had also made in refusing reparation from the German government when she was living in Israel in the 1950s. We were willing to grant that what appeared unspeakably horrible to us might look rosy to the eyes of a small child. What we found harder to stomach was her equally rose-tinted narration of the next phase of her life.

In 1942, as Hitler's army advanced on western Russia, my mother's family were notified that they would be deported again—this time to a refugee camp for displaced Poles in Uzgen, near the border between Uzbekistan and Kyrgyzstan. The train journey to Central Asia, spent in crowded container-carriages without seats, took a week. The food was awful and the sanitary conditions worse. Stella and Nathan both contracted typhoid fever en route; delirious and running a high temperature, she remembered little of their arrival in Uzgen. Her few memories of those first days were of waking intermittently in the camp hospital. Her father, in the adjoining bed, would call out to her, comforting her and singing to her. By the fourth day, her fever had broken. But Nathan was no longer there beside her. She inquired where he was, only to learn from a nurse that he had 'skonchalsya' (passed). Stella didn't quite understand what this meant, and for a long time expected Nathan to pass back. Apparently she waited for weeks at the gates of the camp, and then at the entrance to the mud hut her family had been allocated, convinced that he would reappear.

Nathan's death was a huge blow to Stella's sister Mariska, who at night started to compulsively wet the crib the two girls shared. But it proved a deadly blow to Lola. She had saved the precious family silverware, just as she had saved her sense of superior class breeding by looking down upon the working-class Jewish family in the neighbouring hut; but she was no longer willing to save herself. Lola weakened, sickened, and lost the will to live. By 1944 she too had died.

Decades later, Stella narrated her time in Uzgen as a time of hardship, but also of many joys. The horrors of the train trip from Archangelsk to Uzbekistan were erased and screened by a single defining memory, of the carriage's beautiful blue night-light that would comfort her as she lay awake in the middle of the night. The rest—the starvation, the illness, the nightmares that kept her up and forced her to look for a light in the darkness—she folded and filed away in some other partitioned part of her memory. Uzgen too became, in her account, a happy town. Although she woke up each morning in a pool of her sister's cold urine, with an unfed stomach groaning from hunger, and an unresponsive invalid mother, she liked to tell us that Uzgen was the place with the wonderful market where she learnt to count in Uzbeki and drive bargains; the place with the wonderful one-room school where she and the other students would do sums, run foot races and sing stirring songs to Batushya Stalin (Little Daddy Stalin, who quickly replaced her father as the object of her longing for benevolent paternal care); the place with the wonderful shoe-making Communist neighbours—the Spiegels—who, when her mother died, selflessly took in Stella and Mariska, gave them the coveted sleeping position on their stove and schooled my mother in a utopian left-wing politics that she cherished for the rest of her life.

My sisters and I wanted to believe our mother's stories. And we did. But from an early age we also intuited how much they concealed. The folds of her narratives got unfolded for us in a variety of ways—the panicked cries for her 'Ima!' (Mother!) that she would repeatedly utter at night; her constant aimless whistling when she wasn't talking, as if she needed to silence the din of an orchestra in her head that was always playing and re-playing private symphonies of unwanted noise (ironically one of her favourite whistling pieces was Edith Piaf's 'La Vie En Rose'); the way she would not just constantly sigh but exhale deep, involuntary stutter-shudders through which we could hear the pitchy fume of trauma taking flight from her diaphragm, like a whiff of naphthalene from an old, long-locked cabinet suddenly reopened. Which is to say: my mother's body, as much as her story of her Central Asian Idyll, was like our Chinese chest—a marvellously wrought container stuffed with traumatic secrets that it couldn't help but secrete.

*

Stella's skill in folding didn't stop with the war. In 1946, she and her sister moved to what was then Palestine to live with their mother's brother Joe. After fattening up her emaciated frame at a sanitarium, Uncle Joe sent her to a boarding school in a village of Palestinian Arabs as well as émigré Jews. My mother used to narrate her schooldays, from 1947 to 1951, as a particularly happy time. But these years were marked by a significant rupture. In 1948, the UN Partition Plan for Palestine was implemented, and suddenly my mother found herself on the opposite side of a border from her Palestinian school friends.

The partition of Israel and Palestine marked a division not just in space but also in time. Suddenly people who days earlier had been my mother's beloved comrades were now representatives of a cultural and religious tradition with which 'the' Jews—as if that definite article could ever define the enormity of its fractured, multiple referent—had experienced a supposedly timeless enmity. Stella's memory was partitioned too. When remembering events from before 1948, she would talk with deep affection of her dear Palestinian friends; when remembering events from after that year, she would talk of Palestinians as mortal enemies who wanted to push 'us' into the sea. Over the decades, the misery of Palestinians in the occupied territories of the West Bank and Gaza became the increasingly troublesome secret from which she averted her gaze. She had been trained in averting her gaze from trauma during the war, after all. But her war trauma returned—in the horribly distorted nightmare form of barbaric Palestinians who were threatening to revisit on 'us' the violence the Germans had wreaked. Of course this nightmare, and the attendant Islamophobia my mother cultivated over the decades, effaced the violence of the Israeli state—and the army—in the occupied territories.

In the Chinese chest I recently discovered one photo that was a little out of step with the others. It didn't depict the dead family members who had been lost in the war. It was a rare photo of my mother. She is around twenty, and she still has the gaunt frame of someone who had recently endured years of starvation in Archangelsk and Uzgen. But she is wearing the uniform of the Israeli army, in which she served for two years. She smiles in the photo as she salutes in a patriotic pose.

For some reason, that photo got shovelled into the chest with her other traumatic souvenirs. It never made it into the photo albums that were part of our official family narrative, available for all to look at. I suspect the memory of Israel became traumatic for Stella too. Partly because she came to associate it with loss—the loss of Hebrew, when she migrated to New Zealand and devoted herself to producing a new family with whom she would speak in English; the loss of her Uncle Joe, who died days after I was born (and for whom, along with her father, I was named); the loss of her sister Mariska, who died of cancer in 1965; and, I suspect, the loss of her fantasy that Israel was the vehicle of a glorious socialist future committed, like Batushya Stalin and the Spiegels, to justice for small children exposed to murderous violence.

I inherited from my mother her deep belief in social justice. But it was precisely that belief that led me to question her many inflammatory statements about Palestinians and Muslims—at least the statements that belonged to the post-1948 side of her partitioned memory. The first big fight we had, when I was a teenager, was about the Palestinian Liberation Organization, whom I idealistically supported and whom she saw as Nazis in Arab guise. I reminded her of her stories about her Palestinian boarding-school friends. She then fell into a grim-lipped silence and refused to speak to me for a day. Her silence was broken only by a cascade of horrible stutter-shudders as her exhalations of pain permeated the house. My sisters reprimanded me for being so callous and said I shouldn't be critical of Israel, which my mother so passionately loved.

I'd like to think that my mother's pain wasn't just because I had dared to criticize Israel. Her pain emanated from a more ancient wound inside her, a rent in the fabric of her fantasy of Israel that made it unsustainable even for her. It was a rent produced by the Partition Plan itself. When old solidarities are violently sundered, how can one do anything but fold? Folding a beautiful narrative—of Israel as the socialist redeemer that would spare my mother the traumatic memory of a murdered child, of a murdered childhood—could take her only so far; when its contradictions became manifest, which is to say when she was asked to think about the lot of the Palestinian child-friends the Partition plan had consigned to lives of misery, she folded, or crumpled, under the pressure. And perhaps she had folded long before my argument with her. Which is why that photo of her in the Israeli army had been consigned long ago to the traumatic interior of the Chinese chest.

*

To this day I feel as if Stella's trauma survives in a hidden part of me, as a compulsion that I don't quite understand. My love of that Chinese chest certainly prophesied my infatuation with Asia, where I moved some years ago. And my move has allowed me to forge an imaginative bond with the lost Freud relatives who painted Bengalis, wore kimonos, and posed as pashas.

But why did I move to India, and not another part of Asia? I suspect it is no accident that I moved to a partitioned land, in which an 'I' and a 'P' have been pitted against each other in a tale of timeless enmity that overwrites deep affinities in the past and even the present. Perhaps the need to work through the trauma of my mother's experience of Partition played out, in some obscure way, when I chose to live in a city haunted by memories of 1947. I persuaded myself that in India, and in its rich syncretic traditions, I had found the perfect antidote to the schizoid communal hatreds that had roiled Europe and Israel–Palestine alike. But this antidote was something of a folded crane. It was a beautiful creation, but it hid a secret: that India, whether in British times or in the present, has been only too happy to abide by the principle of divide and rule.

I am struck by the many similarities between India's current situation and that of Europe in the years leading up to the war—and Israel in the years since the war. A right-wing government, voted in by a minority of the electorate on a promise of economic development, has fostered profound communal antagonism. It has cultivated the canard that the majority community it speaks for is in fact an imperilled soon-to-be minority facing enemies from within who breed like cockroaches. It has been aided and abetted not just by its stormtroopers of hate but, most importantly, by everyday citizens who avert their gaze from the atrocities that have been daily unfolding. For nothing has helped the government's cause more than a massive outbreak of folding—folding away the evidence in front of our eyes of ruined institutions of democracy, of suppression of free speech, of thuggery and lynching.

A few months ago, just two blocks from where I live in Delhi, an eight-year-old Muslim boy named Azeem was killed in Malviya Nagar on his way home from the madrasa. In the midst of a scuffle between two groups, Azeem was thrown over a bike by a gang of older Hindu boys from the nearby Valmiki Camp; he died subsequently from internal injuries. The *Times of India*, citing an official statement made to media by Azeem's evidently frightened father, claimed it was not a communal murder but 'just' an accident.

For me, the event summoned the ghost of that ghastly day in Lvov when the Nazis came to the Freud house and murdered Viki. My mother refused to allow that traumatic truth to seep out of the Chinese chest. I understand why. But I have often thought about how and why the neighbours of the Freuds reacted, or didn't react, to Viki's murder. If they knew about it, they presumably stayed silent, as had so many Poles and Germans when they heard about other acts of violence in their midst. Perhaps they stayed silent because they were true believers in the Nazi cause, and they thought: good riddance. Perhaps they stayed silent because they were frightened and didn't want to stir up more trouble. Or perhaps, despite knowing how awful the violence was, they derived a secret pleasure from it—pleasure from belonging to a community supposedly exempt from such awfulness, pleasure from the implicit identification with those who administer rather than receive violence. Maybe they said, to hide such pleasure: it was just an accident. But they doubtless folded away the evidence in front of them, just as my grandfather had when he decided to move his family back to Nazi-occupied Warsaw, just as *The Times of India* did when it uncritically reported that Azeem's father believed his son's murder had no communal dimension.

There are many reasons why we fold in the face of traumatic violence. Folding origami cranes may allow us to dream of a better world in which such violence does not and must not and cannot happen. Which is to say, folding can make a statement against communal hatred. But it can also disavow its temptations and pleasures. That is why, from time to time, we need to endure the stench of naphthalene and sit patiently with what has been folded and stowed in our beautiful containers of secrets. We need to unwrap these secrets to see what we might otherwise want to unsee. Which is to say: we need to unfold our cranes too.

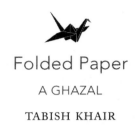

Folded Paper

A GHAZAL

TABISH KHAIR

On roiled and churned-up earth the metallic crane stands,
A post-historic dinosaur that man commands.

Another building rises, skyscraper or mall,
This crane invests the concrete forests of the land.

Around the corner, in a shaded, tasteful room,
Someone puts on the DVD of a rock band

That protests crimes, which on Daily News,
With TV muted, come across, of course, as bland.

The housewife cranes her neck to taste the cooking dish,
Or overhear her neighbours out on an errand.

In this world of windlass, uplift, elevator,
Of derrick, lever, winch, escalator and stand,

In this world of exalting, hoisting, prick up, jack,
Of set up, weigh up, perk up, and their hundred brands,

Where human lives are paper, so easily pulped,
And truth or meaning is nothing but a summand,

Where homicide, murder, rape are reasoned away,
And all emotions are, no, not destroyed, but canned,

In such a world, what use this piece of blank paper
Which I fold into 'crane' and pass unto your hand,

O daughter, son; what use, except this that you too
Will fold it for a child and, folding, understand:

Only the smallest gesture and the gentlest act
Redeem our lives against the falling of the sand.

The Art of War

SUDEEP CHAKRAVARTI

The Inuit have several descriptions for snow. I have a few for razor wire.

Razor wire at dawn, with a touch of marigold and octopus ink. Atop battered walls of a camp, dazzling in the noonday sun. Razor wire touched by the yellow-orange-red of a setting sun. Razor wire with late-monsoon drapery, the upper blades stark, ready to cut flesh, lower blades birthing rain pearls. At another time and another place, drenched in spring dew. The wire taut in sub-zero cold, deceptively softened by snow. Razor wire in tropical heat, the edges seemingly dulled with humidity, slowing the dragonfly that descends onto it for a second's respite. Wire married to peach bougainvillea, within the whorls a beehive, nesting and purposeful. Wire around a camp at dusk, garlanded with empty bottles of alcohol sold cheap to soldiers: patriotic, stress-relieving tonic now emptied to diminish the stealth of the enemy.

The art of war.

Z's place is surrounded by miles of razor wire, each concentric circle leading to his redoubt. The wire reflects a full moon in mellow beige. A slight mist makes the edges softer still. Light and shade makes it look like an installation. You could easily place a string of white origami cranes on it to juxtapose the reality of violence with a quixotic yearning for peace, the kind of work that washes artists in embassy-row Bordeaux and nudges a lucky few towards the next Biennale in Venice.

Wire cocoons Z from harm. So does his flock, who wear muted olive green and matte-black weapons. They shepherd me to him. They keep danger at bay here, ensure freedom from fear. Outside, danger and death are generous, and fear is everything. Z's enemies live there. They don't have razor wire to protect them. They make do with anger.

Troopers are gathered at the porch of Z's sprawling bungalow. Many are clustered in the foyer; jovial, drunk but not disorderly. A celebration. They part as I make my way to the stairs. I nod at them, smiling, and they return the acknowledgement. Then I spoil the effect by showing a raised fist. A symbol of those who are angry, of those they battle. They shrink back. Smiles disappear. If my child were here, she would have told me to behave, save such silly humour for a more eccentric audience.

I have no manners.

'Ah, there you are,' Z says after a brief embrace as I'm shown into the drawing room. There are numerous officers—police, paramilitary in uniform—imbibing the hospitality of the area's reigning policeman. 'Whisky?'

'Scotch?' Z adds, as if it is something more than whisky. 'Wine? We have wine too. Brandy for later.'

'Quite a celebration.'

Z smiles. 'You heard about the operation?'

'Hmm.'

His boys had killed eight rebels early that morning. The dead had been brought out of a nearby forest strung on bamboo poles carried by the paramilitary special forces. CoBRA, they are called. Combat Battalion for Resolute Action. A few carried the weapons of the dead, the motley mix of old assault rifles and ancient Lee Enfield copies were easy to tell apart from the sleek matte-black assault weapons of the troopers—the kind the gentlefolk of Europe sold to us these days alongside fine cheeses and wines, and the gentlefolk of Israel sold to us too, alongside magic irrigation and testaments of survival.

A photographer friend who had arrived first to these jungles, a three-hour drive west of Kolkata, had sent photos to my phone. One image was of a lady among a local band of Maoists, dressed in a summery orange salwar-kameez. Even with a head wound—a trickle of blood and exposed brain tissue—she looked too elegant, too young to be strung up on a bamboo pole, alive or dead. An incongruous animal, not like the tigers and leopards of the old days, hunted and gathered, and ferried so— statements of wayward machismo and, when skinned and cured, interior decoration. Miss Flame-of-the-Forest wasn't in that class. She and her colleagues would in all likelihood cease to be conversation in a day. Perhaps a week.

*

It was the pole.

I have nothing against poles. They make for ergonomic transport in places that are too forested, or too rural, for even a rutted earth road to have reached. And even if they have such roads here in Jangalmahal, the place of jungles, who knows if they are mined or not? Miss Flame-of-the-Forest might well have had her finger on a hair-trigger or two. Until death do us part. The ebb and flow of rebellion.

I choose Johnny Black after being shown a wine label by one of Z's servants. A nervous cabernet sauvignon from the hills not far from Mumbai seems improper for the occasion. Wine doesn't have much of a combat reputation. The servant hands me a glass with about a third filled with whisky and then ceremonially decants water into it.

'Happy days.' I raise my glass to and take a long sip. Z is a connoisseur, so I know the whisky isn't counterfeit.

'Good to see you, chief,' Z mirrors the gesture of several in the room. 'My boys ...' he spreads an arm to include a dozen or so people. He introduces me as a friend from the days when we were a lot younger than we are now, students of history, of politics.

I smile at them all, make a genuine show of a toast to their happiness. As Z moves through the throng, playing host, I place my small backpack next to a sofa and sink into its velour embrace. A portly gentleman with neatly trimmed moustache and cropped hair, the only person in the room besides Z not in uniform, moves a bit to make space for me, spilling some whisky on his tan trousers in the process. He dabs at it with a handkerchief and, then, in a seamless movement, uses the cloth to pat down his moustache. He scrunches the handkerchief into a tight ball. He holds his drink in the other hand. A length of ash from a gold-ribboned acrid cigarette stuck in one corner of this mouth appears about to lose its battle with gravity. He looks like a minor god of dishevelment. I smile at him. He takes that as an invitation to begin a conversation.

'Are you familiar with forensics?' The ash collapses onto his trousers. He lets it be.

'No. I assume you are?'

'Yes,' he seems pleased with my response to his cue. We both speak in clipped tones, as if to reclaim dignity—that matter of spilt whisky and collapsed ash. 'So yes, you see, the chaps don't know the basics of forensics. These railways chaps.'

'And you're . . . ?'

' . . . with CBI. I love forensics.'

'And?' I ask this officer of the Central Bureau of Investigation.

'I'm looking into the incident.' He lets that sink in, takes a sip of his wine, a pull on his fast-burning cigarette. He offers a profile and holds it for a few beats. Then the effort of maintaining his Holmesian gravitas becomes too much. He blurts out: 'I went back to the accident site for the second time today. I was in the hot sun for five to six hours. But it's worth it, you know. I believe each time you go to the scene of the crime you see, you discover, new things.'

'How long do you expect the investigation to take?'

'I'm hoping to wrap it up in three months.'

'Well, you're in a bit of a spot.'

The word was that Maoists had blown up railway tracks not far from Medinipur town, where we were, in western Bengal, about a month ago. The train derailed and collapsed onto adjacent tracks. An oncoming goods train drove straight into it, mangling coaches and people. Nearly a hundred and fifty travellers died. A couple of hundred were injured. Naturally, it had all become political. Those who ruled wished to quickly pin the blame on Maoists. Those who wanted to rule, cynically wished the blame would be pinned on the cynical rulers—and had said as much. The usual horrors.

'Maoists are actually looking to you to exonerate them,' I say. 'They keep insisting they have nothing to do with it. Rogues from one of their fronts do.'

Forensics laughs nervously. He returns to his favourite subject: procedure. 'I'm hoping to establish SOPs for incidents like this, you know, accidents, acts of sabotage.'

Standard operating procedure. I wish there were standard operating procedures for mitigating rebellion. Like empowerment and development and governance. Big words with diminished meaning. I smile with what I hope is encouragement and turn my attention elsewhere. The room is now hazy with smoke. The alcohol-fuelled conversation is several decibels higher than when I arrived.

A CoBRA commander down from Delhi for the operation complains about the cost of living in the capital. By then Z is telling another visitor that he has specific information from communication intercepts: Maoists and their front are indeed behind the disaster. It was a deliberate attack, he says. The leadership of both organizations were aware of the repercussions of first a derailment and the possibility of greater mayhem with oncoming trains on this busy route that links Kolkata with Mumbai. A major statement of revenge for a major attack against them. Z insists it was planned in retaliation for an attack by his boys a couple of days before the butchery from the derailment.

In this savage mini-war over the rights and livelihoods of the poor, the only innocents appear to be the dead. Anyone alive is game. That chilling phrase, collateral damage, is about the unevenness of righteousness, of justice.

In any case, tonight we're celebrating death.

*

It's now a whirl of conversation. Forensics wants to know how Maoists get in touch with people like me—writers, chroniclers. He, the CoBRA commander, Z and I segue briefly into the subject of commando training. They trade gossip about equipment. I show a letter from the Maoists on my notebook computer about their version of the blood on the tracks. Then I copy some music—Dire Straits, Nusrat Fateh Ali Khan and Rolling Stones—onto Z's flash drive.

'We've planned another operation,' Z announces. 'For early morning tomorrow.'

I'm surprised. Here we are, steadily more intoxicated, and an 'op' will soon be under way. The reclaiming of land that the Maoists claim is a liberated zone is gathering momentum. More bodies on poles.

'Don't worry,' Z assures me. 'Everything is in place.'

He then turns to a young officer who enters the room to talk to his superior, the CoBRA commander. Z teases the young officer, a hero of that morning's kills. 'Arrey! You're still sober?'

Then Z begins to share his concerns. He tells me about how he proposed a 5,000-rupee bonus for each person who took part in that day's operation to hunt Maoists. The state's police chief agreed, but seemed to be more concerned about photographs of the slain Maoists than rewarding the troopers.

'I had already emailed him the photos, taken separately—the bodies were in various parts of the morgue, in fact, in two different morgues,' Z fumes. 'The chief kept calling, kept asking for photos of the bodies, all together, lined up, because the home minister wants to see them that way.'

Z says he was too upset to follow up himself, so he asked a junior officer to explain to the chief, so the chief could in turn explain to the home minister of India that they would just have to 'bloody well wait'. The bodies would first have to be collected, then placed in a neat row, elegantly shot to present media-friendly photographs, and then finally returned to the racks in the two morgues.

'Is this what we have to do?' Z explodes. 'Chutiyas. They create the problem in the first place, and we have to clean it all up.'

Someone makes a joke about how it would help if policemen were to learn Photoshop. Z smiles, but he is still very angry.

Forensics and a few others then ask me my views about what I think will happen—with the rebellion in Medinipur, and elsewhere in India.

What can I tell you that you don't already know? I reply. The problems won't go away till corruption and bad governance do. You can kill Maoists and those like them—do what you want, and more will come to take their place. You are no longer policemen. You're firemen who live in palaces of razor wire.

The conversation is now close to maudlin, so Z announces that dinner is served. We stroll into an adjoining room. The food is local, simple yet lavish. Dal, finely cut potatoes with fried bitter gourd, rice, chicken curry, sweetened yoghurt. Dinner for the braves.

As I prepare to leave, Z asks of my plans.

There's a rendezvous to keep with the rebels, who wish to tell me their side of the story. I shall listen. But I care more about what happens to those that both sides claim to be fighting for. The poor and the dispossessed. I've already heard some of it from villagers. Rebels threaten them and harass them. Sometimes the troopers threaten them more. The fortunate are sent off with a caution. Troopers have been making forays deeper into the forest. One patrol broke and torched huts, mixed rice with dirt, beat up villagers, took some away with them after accusing them of either being rebels or sympathetic to the rebellion. Several villagers were frightened into running away.

I had moved constantly, from mud hut to mud hut, and village to village. Residents were afraid to invite police ire for harbouring a writer—an outsider. Also no household could afford to feed me more than once, even a battered aluminium plate of little boiled rice and a smidgen of dal, or puffed rice soaked with water to trick the belly into submission. The better-off among them would add a tiny spoonful of sugar to go with it.

When rice from the harvest ran out somewhere between three to six months, villagers gathered sal leaves from the forest to weave into plates. A thousand plates fetched seventy to eighty rupees.

Everywhere I went there were stories of atrocities. A village woman raped by the vigilantes of the ruling party. A boy beaten and sodomized. A girl threatened, and then ...

Troopers came upon a man in a field who was tending to his cows, Manik, a villager, told me. They called out to him. When he went to them, submissive, scared, they beat him to death.

'I saw him later,' Manik said. 'His ribs were like cotton wool.'

The man's innards had been pulled out of his anus. It isn't unheard of. Stick in a barrel of a gun, twist it, yank it out.

*

'I'm heading in tomorrow,' I tell Z. 'If your chaps come by me in the forest, would you please ask them to be careful about the man with an orange backpack? Ask questions first, shoot later?'

Z smiles.

Korkun / Which Way?

MOHAMMAD MUNEEM

Translated from the Kashmiri by Rumuz e Bekhudi

Ah! I asked the middle, which way?
I am drowning to the left and right, which way?

The darkness is seeking me on every street,
I would grope for the sun, but which way?

When my death-clock strikes, they will look for me
But I am already lost and don't know which way.

I may be no scholar but with fire I let my blood burn my being.
I shrug off their taunts. But, which way?

The white paper crane asked me, 'Who are you? What is Alif?'
I replied, 'I am the artisan of every thought.' Which way?

The Tenant

PRAJWAL PARAJULY

Gangtok, Sikkim

I arrived home to find Deepak, my parents' tenant, close to tears. My parents were evicting him because they were renovating their six-storey building. In my childhood home, everywhere I looked, I saw builders knocking down walls and setting the foundation for a new building to be merged with the existing one. The result would be a structure so unmanageable that my family would have to convert a chunk of it into a hotel. In my Himalayan hometown, upper-middle-class people often occupy the top two or three floors of mid-rise constructions and lease out the lower floors to hotel operators. 'It's the easiest way to free money' is the common refrain.

Deepak rents a convenience store at the road level of my parents' building. Within a few months of moving to Sikkim from the western state of Rajasthan, the shopkeeper had mastered Nepali, the language predominantly spoken here. In the same few months, he had also made himself an indispensable part of the neighbourhood. To his stock of flour, fruit and vegetables, he added noodles, cookies and chocolate. Then there was a photocopy machine. Two years ago, when I expressed disappointment at the lack of ice cream in the store, high-quality ice-cream bars made an appearance. What the neighbourhood demands, Deepak supplies. When racial epithets are thrown his way, he avoids eye contact.

As his business flourished, Deepak rented an apartment in the basement of my parents' building. Soon, his widowed mother moved in with him. The apartment wasn't in great condition. The floors had developed pits and cracks, and the staircase leading to the flat was moss-covered. Deepak and his mother incorporated improvements to their new home and its surroundings. The kitchen sported new countertops, faux wood concealed the uneven flooring, and a Western-style commode replaced the decades-old squatter toilet. Flowers bloomed in mud pots in the balcony. Paper cranes dangled from the balcony ceiling. A wind chime made music at the threshold.

My parents laughed that Deepak's apartment was even nicer than theirs. The comment, though cringe-worthy in its upstairs–downstairs mindset, had some truth to it. My parents liked Deepak. He was just obsequious enough, paid his rent on time and could be trusted with keys when they were away. They also knew Deepak had it good—the rent on his store and apartment, negligible to begin with, stayed the same even five years later—and constantly talked about their generosity when I pointed out they weren't charitable enough. Deepak's mother sometimes sent excellent vegetarian food to my parents. She was often praying. 'She's always calling God,' said my mother, whose place had a cobweb-ridden altar. 'God will find his way to our place, too.'

But Deepak's importance went beyond his pious mother. My father said he went above and beyond the call of duty. Deepak didn't technically have duties—he wasn't an employee—but he made my parents' lives convenient. When their bills needed to be paid, they called Deepak from whatever part of the world they were in. When they needed something that wasn't available in his store, Deepak recruited his mother to man the counter and fetched it for them from another store. 'Not a problem at all,' he'd say. 'It's good exercise for me.' He meticulously documented every purchase my family made from his store and deducted the total amount from whatever rent he owed. I asked my parents if they verified the records. They said they didn't. They trusted him.

And now they were asking Deepak to leave.

A hotelier, conscious of the central location of my parents' building, begged them to lease out to him the lower floors of both the old and under-construction buildings. The money would be several times what Deepak and the other tenants paid. When my parents first told Deepak about the potential conversion, there were tears, so they offered to talk to some neighbours about letting out a flat to him. The market prices, however, were a deterrent. For the price he was paying for a four-bedroom place, he could barely get a two-bedroom in the neighborhood.

When a one-bedroom did materialize, a move—or some semblance of it—happened. Making some show, mother and son lugged a few pots and pans to the new apartment. A driver my mother recruited to spy on them returned with the report that the balcony looked immaculate—the wind chimes, the paper cranes and the flower pots were still there—and nothing like the place of people who were considering a permanent move. Ten minutes later, Deepak and his mother were back. The mother, a vegetarian, had spotted some eggshells by the water pipes in their new home. That wasn't acceptable, she said. They couldn't live in a place that impure. Annoyance overtook whatever sympathy my parents had for their tenants. 'Shopkeepers can't be choosers,' my mother said.

I have asked my parents if they can at least carve out a store space for Deepak from some corner of the newly renovated building. It's his livelihood, I point out. My mother accuses me of being the shopkeeper's mouthpiece. She thinks the West has made me soft. My father confesses that he'd have tried but that he was put off by Deepak's aborted move. 'We don't eat eggs or meat either, and even we wouldn't have been that picky,' he said.

Deepak and his mother continue occupying the apartment and the shop. It's been three months after they were first asked to leave. The builders are working around them, striking down walls in all the rooms except the one mother and son have moved all their possessions to. My parents are away. They hope Deepak will have figured something out by the time they return. On my last day home, I went into the store to get ice cream. Deepak's fridge was empty. He mentioned that he was trying to finish up his stock. 'I may not be here when you come home next,' he said. He called for his mother, who was pottering around in the balcony, to look after the shop and sprinted off.

'We will move back to Rajasthan,' the old woman said to me, her tone accusing, her fingers hard at work on a piece of paper. 'I can get him married to a girl there. The options will be greater.'

'You must be looking forward to that,' I said, not knowing what else to say and headed upstairs.

Five minutes later, Deepak emerged at my doorstep. He handed me a chocolate ice cream. 'Running is good exercise for me,' he said, out of breath.

Boneless Bird

SUMANA ROY

I'm folding paper to give it spine.
Cartilage is an heirloom
that paper doesn't inherit.
Paper—as boneless as the mind.
Between my fingers is a printed map,
stiff, as if it were a slap
of air, hardened from waiting.
Kashmir touches Sri Lanka's forehead,
Bombay embraces a hut in Arunachal.
I keep folding the map—
countries become intimate,
as they can only during war,
keeping their soft parts away;
as if only hardness wins battles.
I am still folding—
a stubble of paper-bones begins to limp.
Flight needs bones, bones and air.
Paper is too skinny, it needs sleep.
Sleep's muscle, its tyranny,
its pavement, its weightless care.

I pause—I want to be gentle,
like eyelashes, like tendril,
but working my fingers is the herd of Time.
Maps cannot hold skies; only its shy water is blue.
So I begin folding again—
I pinch, I stroke, I pat, I blow foo foo.
The bird doesn't fly.
I can't give it the sweetness of air.
Origami can't give it will.
The world flattens its dimensions.
It squats, then falls; air's lost its salt.
Even lifeless birds can't sit still.

The Silence of the Crane

RADHIKA JHA

What strikes me about the origami crane is its silence. Which is why, when I see it, I do not feel glad.

Asifa Bano.

I cannot go there: to what was done to that eight-year-old child. Where it was done. Thinking about it means facing the horror of it, feeling it. Imagining not just how the girl must have felt, but how the killers thought and felt. If I were a poet I would perhaps be able to find a way to approach those feelings, and make sense of them. For in poetry, language can be folded in different ways. And feelings like horror, powerlessness and shame can be remade into something that is moving and powerful. In poetry, as in the case of the origami crane, a page can be given new life and feelings made whole again.

But I am no poet. I just use words to communicate. Sometimes I use them to dissect feelings, or to remember things. Mostly I use words to construct answers to questions that trouble me. I try to understand the world. But in Asifa Bano's case, I fail. For when I attempt to go there, my mind is swamped by revulsion and shame. Then, mercifully, it goes as blank as a sheet of paper.

Nothing silences more swiftly than shame. But silence can be toxic. Like oil preserves a scent, silence preserves pain. Where there is silence, there can be no peace. It is a well-documented fact that those who have been the victims (and survivors) of violence do not like to talk about it. Those who suffered the beatings and public humiliation sessions of the Cultural Revolution in China rarely spoke of it to their own families. Nor did many of those who came out of the concentration camps after the Second World War. Perhaps because of what had been done to them, they felt they had become different. Maybe they thought that even if they tried to explain, those who listened would not understand. Or perhaps they believed that if they put words to their experiences, then they would not survive the pain those memories would bring back. Or maybe they just desperately wanted to pretend that they were like everyone else.

There was a time when words failed even Orhan Pamuk, a Nobel Prize winner. In a moving essay published in the *New York Times*, Pamuk describes how he was unable to talk to his friend, the Turkish Armenian photographer Ara Guler, about what happened to the latter's family during the Ottoman genocide. Pamuk got to know Guler while researching his stories on Istanbul. He'd go to Guler's studio and pore over his photographs of Istanbul in the 1950s and 60s. And they would talk. But never about Guler's Armenian origins, or of his family. But when a Turkish Armenian journalist, Hrant Dink, was assassinated for daring to use the word 'genocide' in an article, Pamuk spoke out and, as a result, received death threats.

Living as a hunted person was not easy. Pamuk says in the essay that he took to spending more and more time in the US, only visiting Turkey for short periods without telling anyone beforehand. In Istanbul he avoided going out as much as possible and didn't contact friends.

Once when he was in the city, the phone in his apartment began to ring. He didn't pick up. The ringing stopped, then began again. Two, three times. Eventually Pamuk did pick up the receiver. It was his friend Ara Guler, the photographer. 'You're back, thank God,' Guler said, 'I'm coming over.' A few minutes later, the photographer arrived. He didn't say a word, just began to cry silently. He sat and cried for twenty minutes, then got up and left. The two men never spoke of the incident.

A person who is forced to swallow injustice becomes a living ghost, slowly hollowed out from the inside. While those who watch injustice and swallow their words also become similarly hollow. Maybe that was why Pamuk spoke out when the journalist Hrant Dink was assassinated even though he knew he would suffer for it. For he knew instinctively, that if he didn't, he would become a ghost.

Words are slippery things. Words like rape can evoke images of desire, frustrated desire perhaps, but desire nonetheless, and hence the word can lose connection with the act it is trying to represent. And so, in speaking the word, the horror of the action is lost and is replaced by something tamer, something society can accept. But rape is never about desire, it is about power, pure and simple. A word like war is associated with courage, bravery and manliness, obscuring the pillage, and death. One of war's favourite weapons is rape and it is used on the weaponless. Where is the courage and bravery in that?

The relationship between the imagination and language is a strange one. Words, or language, rather, is what a child reaches for in order to touch an image inside its head and pin it down to derive greater pleasure from it. Or control it. Words can also be used to tame the imagination so it isn't so frightening any more, as when a child tells its parent about the nightmare it had the previous night. But even as we hurriedly slap words onto those images and feelings and thoughts, what we are reaching for escapes us, mutates and becomes something else. For the imagination cannot be tamed. It is bigger, messier and far more powerful than our puny little words.

Sometimes, however, words can be stronger even than the imagination. They have an uncanny way of reaching directly into the imagination and stirring up thoughts and feelings that we didn't know we had. Paradoxically, it is their intimate connection with the imagination that makes words powerful. Words make us aware of our common humanity, reminding us that inside us, we all hide hopes, feelings, disappointments, yearnings to love, and be loved.

Some words are so powerful that they get imprinted on one's brain. I can never forget the words of a friend, Javed Abidi. 'Indian Muslims chose to be with India,' he once told me. 'We were given a choice and we chose to live in India. Shouldn't that make us more Indian than those who didn't get to choose?' And he chose to be the best Indian, the best human being, he could be—fighting for the rights of the differently abled to jobs and access to public spaces. A wheelchair user from the age of six, he went to university in the US and steered the Disabilities Acts of 1995 and 2016 through parliament. He never let others silence him. Words, he told me, were the only weapons he had to fight the world.

Not long ago, in spite of the fact that I was in a salwar kameez and wearing a bindi, I was refused entry into a temple in Goa. I was told that this was because of my companion—who was a foreigner, a non-Hindu (my husband). 'He's not coming in,' I was quick to reassure them, not understanding the ponytailed pujari's meaning. 'No, you,' he answered, 'You cannot go in.'

Flabbergasted, I asked, 'But why?'

'Because you are with him, you cannot be a Hindu.'

'But I am Hindu, and I am Indian. Here is my passport. This man is my husband.' I replied.

He shrugged, 'This temple is not for you. Go somewhere else. To some other temple.'

Furious, I approached the police to complain. But instead of telling the priest to let me in, they told me instead, '*Randi* [whore], get lost before we put you in jail for soliciting.' It wasn't the first time I had been told that because I had married a foreigner and a Christian I could not be considered a Hindu any more. Normally to this I would reply that one was born a Hindu and died a Hindu, and one could neither 'become' nor 'unbecome' one. But this time, confronted by that policeman, words failed me. My mouth opened and closed like that of a goldfish, and I turned away, feeling as if I would vomit, feeling as if I had been turned into a blank sheet of paper, my identity and sense of belonging, wiped out. I didn't protest because I knew that that policeman had dared to call me a prostitute not because he was crazy but because he could get away with it. He was a part of the state and he knew that the state would protect him.

Many explanations have been offered for why the perpetrators of Asifa Bano's rape did what they did. Some say it was because of money and land, others cite the easy availability of pornography, still others blame religion. But in the end, the reasons are not important, they did it because they thought they could get away with it, because they felt protected. Ultimately, it is the state that decides whose voice (or voices) will be heard. It can give back the power of speech to those that have been silenced, healing wounds that go very deep. Or it can do the opposite, and destroy people by not recognizing that a wrong has been done—silencing them for ever.

It is the sacred responsibility of a government, to protect the weak. If the state reneges on this duty, and tries to enforce the will and beliefs of the majority upon others, then society will disintegrate and nations, cultures, civilization itself will be lost, swept away in a tide of war and violence.

A Bird and the Story of Love

NAMITA DEVIDAYAL

Many hundred years ago, a learned man was wandering around the forest in search of happiness. He was about to enter the Tamasa River to bathe when he saw a beautiful sight and paused. Two tall cranes with crimson necks were engaged in an elaborate dance, wings outstretched, trumpeting and hooting. They twirled and pranced and mimicked each other.

He sat down and shut his eyes. A wave of empathy washed over him. He now saw what the cranes stood for—love and beauty and an interconnected universe.

Suddenly, he heard a terrible plaintive moan and opened his eyes. A hunter had shot at the male bird and, as it fell to the ground, its mate let out a cry of bereavement. The learned man cursed the hunter for his act of violence. He felt the bird's pain. His pathos led to a spontaneous overflow of poetry and what emerged was the first verse of one of the greatest epics of all time.

The poet was Valmiki and the epic he wrote was the Ramayana.

Many years later or earlier—for time can also be circular like the paths of migratory birds—in one of the stories from canonical Buddhist texts, the young Siddhartha nursed an injured sarus crane, his favourite bird, back to health after it had been hunted down by his cousin.

References to the sarus crane (*Grus antigone*) flutter repeatedly into Indian mythology and cultural history, suggesting that this is no ordinary bird. It has always been revered. It is viewed as a symbol of unconditional love and devotion and good fortune, perhaps because it shares a lifelong partnership with its mate. Deemed sacred, it was not hunted and its eggs were often used in traditional remedies. In other parts of the world, like Japan, the paper crane has been folded into a prayer for healing and renewal.

With their expansive migratory trajectories, the many species of cranes transcend borders. The sarus crane, however, is non-migratory. This elegant grey creature is typically found in the marshes and wetlands of North India. It gets its name from 'sarasa', which means 'bird of the lake'. It is the world's tallest flying bird, reaching up to six feet. Over the years, with urban development and hyper-agriculture, freshwater wetlands have been dwindling—and with them, the number of cranes. The sarus crane is now a vulnerable species.

The Mughal emperor Jahangir, known to be a keen naturalist, kept a pair of sarus cranes that he named Laila and Majnu. Writings about him describe how he used to be very protective of the birds; soon after they laid two eggs, Jahangir chased away a large weasel attempting to approach their nest. He would closely observe how they took turns hatching the eggs—Laila would sit on them all night, and after dawn broke, Majnu would scratch her with his beak to indicate that it was his turn. Jahangir even commissioned one of his best-known court artists, Mansur, to paint a miniature of the two cranes.

There is always a point to the stories in mythology. The imagery flaps its silent wings into our imagination, reminding us of who we are and where we come from. Our past is always present—in our collective memory, in our ideas of self. It may not be accidental that the Ramayana, which unravels the human condition with all its mistakes and miseries, begins with the cry of the sarus crane. The story of the righteous man begins with the death of the bird. Perhaps, the gradual extinction of the sarus crane accompanies the slow erosion of our sense of interconnectedness and empathy. The bird's cry continues to haunt us as we traverse a path of hatred and violence—violence against one another and against the planet.

The story of the crane reminds us that there is a symbiotic order in the universe. A grand and highly intelligent network connects all—from the tiny micro-organism to the most sophisticated creature, and past to present. Man is not at the centre of it, however, his behaviour tends to be distorted by a startling hubris. Like the many ironies that flow into the narrative of the Ramayana, man repeatedly discards the humility that might take him back to interconnectedness, back to mud . . . from nothing . . . back to nothing.

And yet, nature continues to work its magic. The sun shines every day, the tides flow with rhythmic precision, a mango seed gives rise to a mango tree and migrating cranes create geometry in the sky at the same time every year. This extraordinarily connected infrastructure is governed by many different laws—which include the laws of nature, the laws of cause and effect. A break in the balance of the natural order has repercussions. When we hurt another being, we are actually hurting ourselves. Was the hunting down of the sarus crane a breakdown of love and mutual empathy?

Have we—the ones who endlessly fold our paper minds into pointless directions—lost our ability to mirror the pain of others, imagining that we are somehow separate from them? We pray silently but we do not hear the cry of the bird, even though it is louder than that day it rang out hundreds of years ago by the Tamasa River. It may be time to revisit the poetry that can resurrect the sarus crane and watch it soar. It may be time, again, for love.

Listen, Papercrane

SRIJATO

Translated from the Bengali by Arunava Sinha

Listen, papercrane
How far can I travel on your back?
Your incomparable whiteness,
This astonishing and unbelievable whiteness, makes me want to
    remember
School uniforms, and with them, the chattering of schoolchildren
It makes me want to remember the white towel folded calmly on
    the bed
Of a busy hospital
Inside which is curled up a newborn girl.

Listen, papercrane
How far can I travel on your back?
When I put my hand on your back and wings, the thick clumps of
    white
Left on my hand remind me of
The hot milk on the table in the morning
Which everyone loved dipping their bread in,
They remind me of the white handkerchief

In the corner of which the young woman had carefully
      embroidered the name
Of her lover the night before he went to war.
These are my memories now.

Tonnes of iron and slabs of cement are my memories now
My memories are gaping buildings with exposed rods and pianos
      with broken teeth
My memories are just ravaged ports and wrecked cities
From whose belly and hands and nose rise nothing but smoke
Which is white no more, not white by any means.
Only your back is white
Listen, papercrane
How far can I travel on your back?

Karwan e Mohabbat

A PERSONAL-POLITICAL JOURNEY

NATASHA BADHWAR

'This is my son, this is where my son was . . . We will not wash this blood.'

Maragatham spoke in Tamil, a language I don't understand, and yet I understood her because she spoke with her entire body. A group of us from Karwan e Mohabbat had entered the small room in which her son had been attacked by a mob of upper-caste people with clubs, logs and axes. There was a flat-screen TV mounted on the wall. Its screen was smashed.

Maragatham, the grieving mother, entered after us. She was wailing and speaking simultaneously. She showed us her son's blood on the mud floor of the room.

Most of us backed off from the spot she indicated, horrified that we had stepped on spilt blood. We moved closer to the walls. She then pointed to blood splattered on the wall, and again I moved away. Speaking loudly to make herself understood, she narrated how her son had been attacked from behind as he sat with a friend: he was killed at that very spot, his head split open.

Kachanatham village in Sivaganga District of Tamil Nadu is 60 kilometres away from the vibrant, bustling city of Madurai. Maragatham is a Dalit woman whose son, Shanmugham, was one of the three men hacked to death by a mob of upper-caste men and women from a neighbouring village. The attackers had gone from home to home, specifically hunting to kill three of the most-educated, highest-earning young men in the village in an attempt to teach the entire Dalit community 'a lesson'. Besides the three who were killed, more than fifteen people were hospitalized with deep cuts, gashes and fractures. Some would be disabled for life.

As we began to move out of the room, Maragatham picked up a log of wood from a pile outside the room and showed us the bloodstains on it: 'This is what they attacked my son with . . .'

I wanted to take the weapon from her hand. I wanted to transfer some calm from my hands to hers. Help her to move away from her abject rage towards a surrender to grief.

But is there a language to console a mother whose son has been bludgeoned to death? Besides her personal tragedy, there was also the historical and structural oppression to understand. A village of Dalits had been targeted by a mob of upper-caste families from neighbouring villages as punishment for having pulled themselves out from extreme penury by pursuing higher education and jobs. Shanmugham was a postgraduate, the second victim was a driver in the city, and the third, a father of a soldier in the Indian Army—when the mob couldn't find the son, who had returned home to get married, they killed his father and looted the home.

As I stepped out of the room that had been the scene of the crime, my eyes first searched for my own fifteen-year-old daughter, Sahar. I needed to see her and yet I hoped that she wasn't too close to our group either. She was standing at a distance. The village of Kachanatham is so neat and colourful that I could have taken a photo-graph of her at that moment and it would have made a pretty picture, reflecting none of the distress we were witnessing as we stood at this site of modern-day inter-caste violence.

Here we were in this moment—one mother, still in shock, beating her chest for a murdered son, and another looking to shield her daughter from the trauma of being confronted by the grief of others.

I'm not quite sure why I have been travelling with my daughter to sites of hate crimes where even I struggle to process the horror of the violence perpetrated. I had asked her if she wanted to travel with Karwan e Mohabbat and she had said yes. She wanted to be a part of the life I was choosing. She wanted to stay close to me. As a parent, I want to both protect my children as well as expose them to the world as it exists around us.

I often wonder what choices I would have made if I hadn't had children. Their presence in my life compels me to leave the home and become an activist. By travelling and working with Karwan e Mohabbat, I am responding to the rise of right-wing Hindutva in India and its impact on vulnerable communities and minorities. I must show my children that we are standing up against injustice, that we challenge the politics of hate. That we reach out to victims at a time when they have been abandoned by the state as well as society.

When did my understanding of family and country and my role in both become so intertwined with each other? I surprise myself, both with the depth of my own distress as well as my quiet commitment to transmute my helplessness into action.

*

In the autumn of 2017, Harsh Mander, a writer, teacher and human rights worker, announced the founding of Karwan e Mohabbat (Caravan of Love), a journey of atonement, solidarity and conscience to visit people who had been victims of hate attacks and to offer them the support they needed towards justice, livelihood and healing.

My husband and I had felt an instant connect when we first heard of this civil-society initiative, which had launched with an online crowdfunding appeal. A few weeks later, I joined a group of people who had all responded to Mander's call to travel across parts of India hit hardest by lynchings. Among our group were writers, photographers, educators, journalists, social workers, activists, scientists and a group of young men studying to be Catholic priests.

'The purpose is twofold,' Mander had written in his crowdfunding appeal. 'To respond to the everyday fear of Muslims, Dalits and Christians and the worrying silences of the majority.'

One of the first prominent cases of hate crime had been that of the lynching of Mohammad Akhlaq in his own home in Bisara village, Dadri, Uttar Pradesh. On 28 September 2015—over a year after the Narendra Modi-led Bharatiya Janta Party (BJP) had come to power in India—a mob attacked Akhlaq's family in response to an announcement made in a temple claiming that they had slaughtered a calf to consume beef. Among other weapons, the attackers had used a sewing machine from the home to attack both the father and his son. Akhlaq died and his son was admitted in hospital with serious head injuries.

Dadri is less than 10 kilometres away from my home on the outskirts of Delhi. Its news had triggered a visceral sense of dread for what had been unleashed in Indian society.

Over the next few months and years, multiple attacks were reported on Muslims and Dalits, many of them accompanied by gory videos of the lynchings. A teenage boy called Junaid Khan was beaten to death on a train when he was returning home after shopping for Eid in Delhi's Chandni Chowk area. Pehlu Khan, a dairy farmer, was lynched in Alwar by self-styled 'gau-rakshaks'—cow vigilantes—when accused of transporting cattle for slaughter, despite carrying papers to prove that he had bought milch cattle to rear in his own home. In Jharkhand, Mazlum Ansari and a 15-year-old Imteyaz Khan were returning home from a cattle fair when they were attacked and hung from a tree by men belonging to the Bajrang Dal, the youth wing of the Rashtriya Swayamsevak Sena (RSS), the right-wing, Hindu nationalist outfit that is regarded as the parent organization of the Bharatiya Janta Party. The victims were poor cattle traders who made ends meet by buying young calves and selling them again after rearing them to adulthood. In Mangalore, Harish Poojari was stabbed 14 times and his intestines pulled out, only because the attackers—again from the Bajrang Dal—mistook him for a Muslim when he was riding pillion on a motorcycle that was being driven by his Muslim friend who was wearing a skullcap.

A disturbing nationwide pattern had begun to emerge. Fuelled by the anti-Muslim rhetoric and upper-caste Hindu supremacist posturing of the leaders of the ruling BJP, more and more Indians were beginning to justify hate violence perpetrated on innocent citizens of minority communities. Social media and WhatsApp groups circulated fake news, Islamophobic opinions, and a renewed pride in being Hindu, based on a crude reimagination of history and mythology. The increasing intolerance towards, and disregard for, liberal, secular values and a scientific temper was palpable.

On the political stage of the country, the constitutional promise to protect and nurture the most vulnerable communities and people was being disregarded by those in power—the very people whose role it is to enforce the commitment.

'How culpable are we when our brothers and sisters are burnt and lynched and we stand by? We need to interrogate the reasons for our silences . . . we need our conscience to ache. We need it to be burdened intolerably,' Mander would repeat, trying to frame the discourse to include the culpability of silent bystanders.

In our second-oldest child's diary I found a line that read like her own one-line bio—'I am a Muslim, a Hindu, an Indian. And I love Harry Potter.' She signed it with her name, Aliza.

The innocent directness of the statement moved me so much I had taken a photo of the page. I remember having a strong sense of being an Indian as I was growing up, but those decades had also been a time of singing patriotic songs in school, celebrating nationhood via Independence and Republic Day broadcasts on Doordarshan and being raised by a generation who had witnessed the freedom movement and been part of the brick-by-brick building of a new India.

The child of an inter-faith marriage, Aliza had observed life around her and picked for herself the identities that felt like home to her. After Akhlaq was lynched, I wrote a column in *Mint Lounge* that was titled 'Can Aliza's India Survive?'

For how long would the child be allowed to claim her multiple identities with safety and dignity?

*

Over the course of the next two years, the Karwan continued to travel across multiple states, making at least one journey every month and often making repeat visits to the homes of survivors to help them navigate legal processes and follow up on their psycho-social welfare. The team expanded to include lawyers, researchers and young film-makers. We started creating a long-term media archive to preserve the details of the crimes and their impact on lives. We also began to make and disseminate films to document the hate crimes, to establish patterns and to record the testimonies of survivors as well as the responses of others affected.

We quickly realized that these were not just stories of tragedies. These were also accounts of great resilience and of truth telling. Of people who not only refused to be defeated but also offered hope and solace to those who came to mourn with them.

The journeys made many of us in the team confront our self-imposed limits and interrogate our commitment to go beyond our own comfort zone. Do I have the emotional stamina to stay with the tragedy and its consequences on the family who are struggling to come to terms with it? Can I resist the distraction that the privilege of my class, caste and location bestows on me, even for short periods of time?

In my earlier career as a video journalist in broadcast news, I had repeatedly found myself covering massacres, riots, bomb blasts, accidents and other incidents of death and loss. In retrospect, I know that my camera equipment and the rigour of functioning as a professional would help to insulate my colleagues and me temporarily from the horror of what we were witnessing. After a decade of chasing the news, the dissonance created by the lack of permission to feel our feelings and our increasing disconnect with the people whose lives we were reporting left me feeling burnt out. I felt that I was betraying both the people I was representing in my work as well as my own self. I needed to leave what I had loved so deeply to recover and restore my core.

A decade later, I was going back to similar scenes of crimes, listening to people narrate the minutest of details. This time there was no video camera in my hands, no shots to compose or deadline to chase and abundant permission to listen deeply and empathize. There were others in the team showing the way and helping make sense of the mindlessness of the crimes and the impunity of the perpetrators.

Yet, the frustration of being nothing more than a drop in the ocean continued to bog me down. I know that my main contribution, apart from physically holding and consoling survivors, is to write their stories. To make films that document the systematic targeting of vulnerable communities and castes to push them back towards penury, helplessness and voicelessness. To reveal the collusion of the state and ruling classes and to hold them accountable.

I have cried a lot, but not typed enough. I have yet to write the stories that have hit me the hardest in my gut.

There is a way to sublimate my personal distress into strength and power—I know that. There is a way to out-walk the depression that clings to me like a weight around my ankles, slowing me down, holding me back. I don't have enough words to describe horror, pain, outrage. But I must break through the wall of my own inarticulateness.

*

'Empathy is first and foremost an act of imagination,' Mander often reiterates. Compassion is an integral part of human nature but our privileged upbringing trains us not to care. We can unlearn the apathy that we have internalized.

Everywhere we travel, we almost always find ourselves addressing community gatherings. Every time I come face to face with the discomfort of breaking my own silence, I find that I don't have to think too hard to frame sentences. The connections are already there, I just have to step out of my own way and let the words flow. The boundaries are artificial. There is power in reaching out.

'My name is Natasha Badhwar and my husband's name is Mirza Afzal Beg,' I began, as I found myself facing a predominantly Muslim male audience in Kandhla, a small town, or what is called a 'kasba' in Shamli District of Uttar Pradesh. 'My father is called Trilok and my father-in-law is Ashfaq. The story of this land is the story of my family.'

We were in a Muslim-majority area that had seen a robust participation in the Revolt of 1857 as well as the later freedom struggle against British colonization. Leaders from the community had shared with us earlier in the day that while caste rivalries between Jats and Dalits have always been sharp-edged in this area, communal violence was a new and manufactured phenomenon. Karwan members and volunteers had organized an Aman Sabha—a peace meeting to talk and to listen.

I shared the Partition stories from both sides of my family. How my husband's grandparents in Ghazipur in east Uttar Pradesh had been cut off from their eldest son who had chosen to hold on to his government job in Chittagong when the country was divided in 1947. When he began to die of cancer in the 1970s, his mother could not get a visa to meet her own son, who had now settled in Karachi. A village in Uttar Pradesh mourned for one of their own that they could no longer reach out to.

I spoke about my Hindu grandparents who had left behind their home in Lahore and crossed over with young children to start life anew. Despite my grandfather's success in the transport business, he died prematurely. The stress and trauma had caught up with him. I mentioned the names of my own children—the great-granddaughters of these two families—who are a symbol of a land trying to heal from the wounds of its past. We are the adults who must turn the tide away from hate.

I don't always like to mention that my husband is a Muslim or that my children have a mixed identity. I feel defensive about the deduction that I am invested in this work because the threat perception is more real for my own family and those who I love. I want to raise my voice and say that it doesn't matter. The atrocities, the injustice, the horror of what we are witnessing does not amplify or diminish according to the location in which we, the witnesses are situated.

As a woman, I have never cared to belong to any religion. I don't accept the traditional hierarchies of the regressive, patriarchal structure of any religion as it is practised.

Yet, I have begun to often publicly proclaim my Hindu identity when I speak to people in communities. I position myself in the majority community and speak to other Hindus from there. I am an upper-caste urban Hindu and that removes me from harm's way. But is this the kind of Hindu you and I want to be? Is this the kind of Indian we collectively want to be?

*

Why is it so hard to write this essay? I change fonts on the page. I minimize the document on my computer screen in the daytime and resolve to write at night. I am too uncomfortable at night to type at my desk. I carry it with me when I am travelling on the Karwan e Mohabbat journeys, thinking I will write when the experience and emotions are raw and live. I return home with a growing shame and guilt that I am continuing to neglect writing this essay.

Is it too vast for me to process? Is there trauma to relive that I am avoiding? I know for certain there is some kind of imposter syndrome. Who are you to tell the story of others who have suffered unimaginable violence, an inner voice nags me. What are you going to do, bleed your heart onto this page? How will that help anyone who has lost the only earning member of their family?

From across the country, the news of lynchings and hate crimes continue with scarcely a pause. A Goa-based musician on a field trip in a tribal area in Assam was lynched on suspicion of being an outsider with malicious intentions. In vain, he screamed the names of his upper-caste Hindu parents to try to convince his attackers that he is not a Muslim. In Manipur, Farooq Khan, recently returned from Bangalore with a fresh MBA degree was accused of stealing a two-wheeler, attacked by a mob in the presence of police personnel and his slow, painful death recorded on mobile phone cameras. Closer to Delhi, there are yet more video recordings of hate crimes reported in Hapur, Mewat, Saharanpur and Gurgaon.

There are few condemnations by those in power. In most instances, the administration files criminal cases against the murder victims and perpetrators roam free, often feted by politicians and protected by their own communities. Families of victims find themselves isolated and abandoned, struggling to deal with their new reality. Most of them have no means to claim compensation from the state and are unable to negotiate with local police and courts.

I write a reported piece on the lynching of Rakbar Khan in Mewat for a narrative journalism magazine. His bereaved wife had been lying in bed, almost unresponsive, unable to sit up straight when Mander and I visited their home within a few days of the incident. Her daughters are the same age as mine. There is a photo of Rakbar—viral on social media—that shows the man alive when the police had reached the scene of the crime and taken him into custody. Yet, he died within hours. There is callousness and collusion on the part of those whose duty it was to rescue the victim.

I have a near meltdown as I spend a weekend negotiating with overworked desk editors about small details like photos and headlines. I am raging at my own powerlessness. 'A man has died, his family is destroyed and we are obsessing over photo captions . . .' I cry to myself in a corner of my room. There are guests and children at home, plans being made to attend a wedding. Friends try to hold on to me till I recover.

What am I pretending to be? I know I am harassed most by own self-doubt and internalized judgement. There is survivor's guilt. Discomfort with my own privilege. There is a nagging sense of never having done enough. I tire myself out and shut down to recoup my energy.

At some point I will have to deal with the wounds within me, so I am parking them here for now. Acknowledging on the page that they are there and that they influence how I function. They demand healing.

As the journeys continue, I get more opportunities to know myself better. I also see a quieter, calmer side of me. One who speaks up in groups and is no longer paralysed by attacks of shame. There is also the high of solidarity, of support, of the memories of forming connections with each other.

The more grief we confront, the more we expand our ability to experience happiness, fraternity and friendship with the people we meet.

*

At home, there is unexpected good news.

My brother and sister-in-law, parents of eleven-year-old twins, are expecting a baby. At a phase in our lives when my peers and I have begun to question whether we are able to do justice to the childhoods of our adolescent offspring, the news of a new baby in our midst feels like a reset button has been pressed in our lives.

We cannot afford to be weary and cynical. She deserves fresh energy from us. She will bring a fresh energy and a light-hearted happiness into the extended family.

As my sister-in-law's pregnancy advances, our firstborn daughter continues to accompany me quietly on many of the Karwan e Mohabbat journeys—to Gujarat, Tamil Nadu, Karnataka, Assam and Orissa. At home, Aliza, now aged 14, learns to manage her anxieties about the world and the risks she often worries her mother is taking. Our youngest child, Naseem, begins to fold paper cranes to welcome the baby. Origami is part of the curriculum in her Waldorf school and our home is dotted with delicate paper butterflies, frogs and cranes.

To mark the birth of her new cousin, she folds the smallest paper crane imaginable. It is so small that I am afraid I might disfigure it when I hold it between my fingertips. We place it delicately on Naseem's palm and take photos. She has made a family of cranes—parents, adolescent twins and a newborn baby.

This unexpected gift of a new baby has transformed our extended family and brought us back into a group huddle after years. The brain functions best when it is hopeful. Acting as if we have hope revives our spirit and eventually averts our own surrender to despair. The baby is named Aditi—boundless.

Aditi has arrived in a world in which Maragatham is mourning for her young son who was hacked to death. The healthiest psychological response to alarming information is action. Slowly, persistently, collectively, we have to continue the work of healing and resistance. With hope, optimism, even naiveté, if need be.

NOTES ON CONTRIBUTORS

An award-winning journalist, **Pallavi Aiyar** has worked as a foreign correspondent for two decades reporting from China, Europe, Indonesia and Japan. She is the author of several books including *Smoke and Mirrors*; *Chinese Whiskers*; *Punjabi Parmesan* and *Babies and Bylines*.

Tishani Doshi is an award-winning poet, novelist and dancer. Her most recent books are *Girls Are Coming Out of the Woods*, shortlisted for the Ted Hughes Poetry Award, and a novel, *Small Days and Nights*.

Salil Tripathi is the author of three works of non-fiction and writes for newspapers in India and abroad. He chairs PEN International's Writers in Prison Committee. Born in Bombay, he has been a correspondent in Singapore and Hong Kong, lived in London, and is currently based in New York.

Anjum Hasan is the author of the novels *The Cosmopolitans*; *Neti, Neti*; and *Lunatic in my Head*; the short-story collections *A Day in the Life* and *Difficult Pleasures*; and a book of poems *Street on the Hill*. Her books have been shortlisted for the Sahitya Akademi Award, the Hindu Best Fiction Award and the Crossword Fiction Award, and she is a winner of the Valley of Words Award for Best Fiction.

Janice Pariat is a columnist, soap-maker and award-winning writer, currently living in Delhi, where she also teaches at Ashoka University. Her most recent novel *The Nine-Chambered Heart* was published in 2018 and has been translated into twelve languages.

Ranjit Hoskote is a poet, cultural theorist, translator and curator. He is the author of thirty books, including *Jonahwhale* (Hamish Hamilton, 2018), *I, Lalla: The Poems of Lal Ded* (Penguin Classics, 2011) and *Confluences: Forgotten Histories from East and West* (with Ilija Trojanow; Yoda, 2012).

'**Shovon Chowdhury** is a slightly disturbed Delhi-based author. Due to a massive failure of quality control, his first novel, *The Competent Authority*, was shortlisted for a wide variety of prizes.'

Gopika Jadeja is a bilingual poet and translator, writing in English and Gujarati. Her poetry and translations have been published in journals and magazines like *The Wolf*, *Wasafiri*, *Asymptote* and *Indian Literature*. She has recently completed a PhD on Gujarati Dalit poetry and is working on translations of poetry from Gujarat into English.

Samrat Choudhury is a columnist and author, and a former editor of newspapers in Delhi, Mumbai and Bengaluru. He tweets as @mrsamratx.

Veena Venugopal is the author of two works of non-fiction—*The Mother-in-Law* and *Would You Like Some Bread With That Book*. Her job as an editor helps pay the bills while she works on her first novel.

Annie Zaidi is the author of *Prelude to a Riot*; *Gulab*; *Love Stories #1 to 14* and *Known Turf: Bantering with Bandits and Other True Tales*, as well as the co-author of *The Good Indian Girl*. She has edited *Unbound: 2,000 Years of Indian Women's Writing* and *Equal Halves*.

Swaminathan S. Anklesaria Aiyar is the consulting editor at the Times of India Group and a research fellow at the Cato Institute, Washington DC. He was the editor of two of India's leading financial dailies: the *Economic Times* and the *Financial Express*.

Gurmehar Kaur is a social activist and author who was featured in *Time* magazine's 'Ten Next Generation Leaders' in 2017. She is currently pursuing a Master's degree in modern South Asian studies at the University of Oxford.

Poet, editor, translator, publisher and curator of the annual Odisha Art Literature Festival, **Manu Dash** has published 25 books in Odia and English, including his recent poetry collection *A Brief History of Silence*.

Jonathan Gil Harris is a writer and teacher based in Delhi. He is the author of many books, including the bestselling *The First Firangis: Remarkable Stories of Heroes, Healers, Charlatans, Courtesans and Other Foreigners Who Became Indian*.

Poet, novelist and critic, **Tabish Khair's** most recent publication is the novel *Night of Happiness*. An Indian citizen, he teaches in a university in Denmark.

Sudeep Chakravarti is a chronicler of conflict and conflict resolution, and an award-winning author of several books of narrative non-fiction and fiction. His latest book is *Plassey: The Battle that Changed the Course of Indian History*.

Mohammad Muneem Nazir is a poet, singer and songwriter who writes in Kashmiri and Urdu. He is co-founder of the band Alif, as well as winner of the IRAA award for the single 'Like a Sufi' in 2017, and also the recipient of the eighth Dada Saheb Phalke film festival award in 2018 for the single 'Lalnawath'.

Rumuz e Bekhudi, a member of the prestigious Sangam House's Simurgh Project, is a multilingual poet and translator based in Kashmir.

Prajwal Parajuly is the son of an Indian father and a Nepalese mother. He is the author of *The Gurkha's Daughter* and *Land Where I Flee*.

Radhika Jha is the author of *Smell; The Elephant and the Maruti; Lanterns on Their Horns* and *My Beautiful Shadow*. She is currently working on her fifth book, set in Japan, titled *The Hidden Forest*.

Sumana Roy is the author of the nonfiction book, *How I Became a Tree* as well as *Missing: A Novel* and *Out of Syllabus: Poems*.

Namita Devidayal has written three books—*The Music Room*; *Aftertaste* and *The Sixth String of Vilayat Khan*. She is a journalist with the *Times of India* and co-director of the Times Litfest, Mumbai. She lives in Mumbai.

Srijato is a poet, lyricist and novelist from Kolkata, who writes in Bangla. He has won several awards, including the Ananda Puraskar, Krittibas Puraskar and Bangla Academy Puraskar for his poetry, as well as the Filmfare East Award for his lyrics.

Arunava Sinha translates Bengali fiction and poetry into English. His recent and forthcoming translations include Bani Basu's *Moom*, Ashoke Mukhopadhyay's *A Ballad of Remittent Fever* and Akhteruzzaman Elias's *Khwabnama*.

A writer and filmmaker, **Natasha Badhwar** is the author of *My Daughters' Mum* and *Immortal For a Moment*. She leads the media team at Karwan e Mohabbat, a civil-society initiative that supports victims of hate crimes and counters the discourse of hate with love and solidarity.